DoGs just wanna have FuN

Also by Jass Richards

This Will Not Look Good on My Resume

The Road Trip Dialogues

The Blasphemy Tour

License to Do That

DoGs just wanna have FuN

Jass Richards

Magenta

Published by Magenta

Magenta

Dogs Just Wanna Have Fun

ISBN 978-1-926891-52-1

Cover design by Elizabeth Beeton and Jass Richards
Cover images by Jass Richards
Formatting and interior book design by Elizabeth Beeton

www.jassrichards.com

Library and Archives Canada Cataloguing in Publication

Richards, Jass, author
Dogs just wanna have fun / Jass Richards.

Short stories.
Issued in print and electronic formats.
ISBN 978-1-926891-52-1 (pbk.).--ISBN 978-1-926891-53-8 (ebk.).--ISBN 978-1-926891-55-2 (pdf)

1. Dogs--Fiction. I. Title.

PS8635.I268D63 2014 C813'.6 C2013-908064-3
C2013-908065-1

for dogs everywhere

with special thanks
to the ones I have known

especially
chess, Taffi, Buddy, and Bailey

TABLE OF CONTENTS

1

WALKING (WITH) THE DOGS

It all started because I kept getting fired. I'd had over a dozen jobs in the last year and lost every one of them. Though 'lost' probably isn't quite the right word. It sounds so...sad.

So I thought I'd create my own job. I decided I'd become a dog walker. Well, I was already a dog walker. I took Kessie for a walk several times a day. As she, to all appearances, took her bright green tennis ball for a walk. Don't leave home without it.

And now we had Snookums too. Snookums was just a little baby. A sweet little bundle of licks and kisses. About twelve weeks. And six pounds. She (too) had me wrapped around her little paw. Her teeny little paw with the still baby pink pad. The one she lifted when she wanted me to carry her. In the snuggly sling thing I wore for just that purpose.

So, since I was already going for walks with Kessie and Snookums, what I meant was that I'd decided to become a *professional* dog walker. I'd *get money* to do it. I wouldn't do it any better, mind you. I'd just get paid for it.

I put up signs in the neighborhood, and within a week I'd received three responses. Not from the dogs, of course. As far as they were concerned, they could walk on their own. Most had been doing so pretty much since birth. Which is more than I can say for members of my own species.

So a week later, Kessie, Snookums, and I were on our way to pick up Hunk. A male doberman who was aptly named, but not quite as big as his owner wanted him to be. Nor, he indicated, with gesture and facial expression, as smart. After a few days with Hunk, however, I decided the guy was wrong—and realized it's true: it takes one to know one.

While we stopped to get Hunk, Kessie was patient, but indifferent. After all, she had a bright green tennis ball in her mouth. As for Snookums, she peeked with curiosity from the safety of her snuggly thing. At the dog! The BIG DOG!! She squiggled in excitement. She likes nothing better than being part of a pack. Even if it is from the safety of her snuggly thing.

Our next stop was to pick up Little Miss Bo Peep. Little Miss was a female standard poodle. A very white, very clean, standard poodle. So she had outgrown the 'Little' but not the 'Miss'. Where the 'Bo Peep' came from, I have no idea.

Kessie was again patient, Snookums was again excited, and Hunk was—interested.

Next stop was for Spunky Doo. Half hound, half clown. Unlike Hunk's architect and Little Miss Bo Peep's lawyer, both of whom didn't have time to walk their dogs, Spunky Doo's owners *did* walk him. In the morning before they went to work, in the afternoon as soon as they got home, and again at night. And still Spunky Doo was a one-dog demolition crew. So the idea was that if I walked him during the day, he'd work off the excess energy he'd been channeling into deconstructing the living room furniture. Or maybe the walk would alleviate the boredom that led to his daytime amusements. In any case, if Spunky Doo wasn't *in* the house, he couldn't wreck the house. No argument there.

SO THINGS WERE GOING rather nicely. We even had the multiple leash thing worked out. After experimenting with several arrangements, we discovered we did best with Hunk and Little Miss together in my left hand, Kessie and Spunky Doo in my right, and Snookums mostly in her snuggly thing. I set her down occasionally, but there was a real concern that she'd get landed on, by Spunky Doo, by mistake. Also, of all the paws she saw from her vantage point at ground level, she wasn't quite sure yet which ones were hers.

Spunky Doo was clear on that point, but it didn't seem to help. I must have put his harness on a dozen times. But still he didn't seem to get it. *This* paw goes in *this* hole? Or *this* one? And my head goes *here*? No, here. No, wait, I remember. My head goes here. I was paying only half attention once, got him all harnessed up, clipped the leash on, and was set to go, Hunk and Little Miss in my left, Snookums in her snuggly, and Kessie and Spunky Doo in my—wait a minute—Spunky Doo was grinning at me from ear to ear as he was—facing me. That's not right. (He probably would've walked backwards too.)

One day, although I'd noted quite clearly on my signs that I was offering to walk *dogs*—'course it could have been *because* I'd noted that quite clearly—a cat decided to join us. It sauntered over to us, took the lead, and, well, led. Hunk, big male dog as he was, felt *compelled* to compete with it. I had no idea what the object of the competition was. Let alone the standards of judgment. I suspect Hunk was clueless on this matter as well, because he kept losing. I thought it likely the standards kept changing. The cat would strut, Hunk would strut, then the cat would give him a scathing look, and he'd know he'd lost. He'd hang his head and put his tail between his legs. Then the cat would resume strutting, Hunk would resume strutting, and he'd lose again. Each time, Hunk would stick his chest out even further, lift his head even higher—and lose even more dismally. Little Miss was not impressed.

We eventually got to the dog park. "Well, here we are at the *dog* park," I said pointedly to the cat. It gave me a scathing look. I gave it the finger and took a moment to decide which way we wanted to go. Some guy walking three dogs approached me, as I stood there with my five, and, after a moment, said "You've got me beat!" Took me a minute, but then I understood—and introduced him to the cat.

AFTER A FEW WEEKS, we all got tired of the dog park. And frustrated with the whole leash thing. There was really no need to keep anyone leashed except Hunk, and that was only because people freaked out when they saw an unleashed male doberman. And Spunky Doo, because he'd take off. In a heartbeat. Not because he didn't like being with us. But just because he had to be everywhere at once. People kept giving me dirty looks when they realized Little Miss and Kessie weren't leashed. Even an unleashed Snookums was cause for serious moral disapprobation. So I decided it was time for a field trip.

To a field. There was one near my place—it was relatively large and surrounded by quiet streets. The dogs could get some real running time and still be safe. I hadn't used my car for a bit, so I went out and opened all the doors to get rid of the stuffy smell. Shook out the dog blanket in the back seat and moved out a few things to make room for Hunk, Little Miss, and Spunky Doo. Then I went back in the house to get Kessie, who was all set with her tennis ball in her mouth, and Snookums, who was now seven pounds.

When we got back out to the car, there was a large dog sitting in the passenger seat, nice as you please, ready to go. Looked like a lab cross. Blond. Kessie took one look and bounded into the car all happy to meet him. That doesn't usually happen. Snookums is the social butterfly. Kessie isn't interested in other dogs. She's got her tennis ball. I followed her into the car and checked his tag. Chum. Phone number, no address. I pulled out my cell phone and called his people, but there was no answer. Well, okay, sure you can come. He thumped his tail.

We picked up Hunk, then Little Miss, then Spunky Doo. All three got into the back seat, Hunk claiming the open window on the driver's side, Spunky Doo, the one on the passenger side. Little Miss sat primly between them. Kessie had claimed the prime spot—my lap, with her nose to the air vent, my hand wrapped around her chest, holding her steady as she leaned into it, breathing in a kaleidoscope—and Chum was in the seat beside us. Snookums was—car sick. All over Little Miss. She was not impressed. Hunk licked it off her. Eew. That impressed her.

Ten minutes later, we pulled into the field. Yippee!! Woohoo!! Free!! We're free!! We're free at last!! Thank God Almighty, we're—yeah, yeah. Kessie knew the score because we'd been coming here for years. She carefully put her tennis ball into my hand, then assumed her ready position—sprinter's crouch in the starting blocks. I threw the ball and she raced after it, leaving Asafa Powell or whoever currently held the 100M record in the dust. (And she's not even black.) She trotted back with it, put it snugly into my hand, and got ready again. I threw it again. She raced after it, trotted back with it, put it into my hand again. We could do this for hours. Had done so, on many occasions.

Snookums, on the other hand, wasn't much of a ball chaser. She'd run after it, but when it stopped, she stopped. She wasn't much of a tug of war player either. Actually I hadn't yet figured out how to play with her. Didn't know what her natural desires were. But today, she trotted off without hesitation, and did whatever it is that puppies do in fields—chase butterflies and birds or something.

Chum, in the meantime, had found one of the million tennis balls Kessie had lost there. Turns out he was a ball dog too. No wonder it was love at first sight. Especially since he understood he was *not, ever,* under *any* condition, to go after Kessie's ball.

Hunk and Little Miss were pretty much sidewalk and dog park dogs, so we were a bit uncertain at first about what to expect. They ventured a short distance away, then returned to me when I called; I told them what good dogs they were. They ventured out again on their own, returned when I called, and were again told that they were very good dogs. Thus assured, they were soon running full out to the end and back with relative abandon.

Spunky Doo needed no such assurance. He was beside himself with joy. (And already convinced he was a good dog.) He didn't know where to go first. So he tore off to the right, then tore off to the left, then ran straight ahead, then turned, kicking up dust, and ran straight—into me. Knocked me flat on my ass. Kessie carefully put her tennis ball into my hand.

Then I saw my sweet little Snookums in the distance playing with something. Tossing it in the air, again and again, so—gleefully. It was bigger than a butterfly. It was bigger than a bird. It was—a rabbit. An ex-rabbit. (I hoped.) She trotted over to me, carrying it, more or less, in her mouth, tripping over whatever was trailing—eew. She had blood, and whatever, all over her muzzle. But she was oh so very proud. Baby's first kill. She was not, no way, giving it to me, mind you—she was just showing me. She wasn't done playing with it yet. My gruesome little Snookums.

Meanwhile, Spunky Doo was still tearing around in all directions, right, left, forward, backward, up—what? Did he just—? Yes, he did. He just chased a squirrel up a tree. Scrambled right up the trunk to the first branch, and then lunged up—to the second branch—made it! Oh. He looked down. That's a bit of a jump. Now what, he looked at me. Yeah. Duh. Now what. For a second it looked like he thought about jumping down. NO! Damn it, what was the word for 'Stay!' his owners had taught him? It was something I knew I'd never remember in an emergency. "Stay! Stay Put! Freeze! Don't Move! Wait! Be Still!"—ah—"Remain Immobile!" He looked at me, and then, somewhat impossibly, lay down on the branch, legs dangling on either side.

I looked around. And saw no ladders nearby. Not that Spunky Doo would know how to use one. I sighed, then pulled out my cell phone and dialed 911.

"What is the nature of your emergency?"

"I have a dog stuck in a tree."

"I'm sorry. You have a *dog* stuck in a tree?"

"Yes."

"Name, please."

"Spunky Doo."

The operator paused.

"I meant *your* name."

"Oh, sorry." I gave my name, phone number, and location. By now, the other dogs had gathered around. This was too good to miss. An opinion validated when they heard the firetruck siren. And saw people streaming out of their houses to come see.

The truck pulled into the field near the tree. An extra-full crew of firefighters disembarked, took in the situation, then tried hard not to laugh. They held a brief consultation. And took some photographs.

Then they decided that getting Spunky Doo into the basket on the end of the crane might be tricky. So the plan was, instead, to ease him over the branch into a net which they would then lower with the crane.

They positioned their truck.

"Remain immobile!" I shouted up at Spunky Doo. They all looked at me. I shrugged.

Once up there, they realized that one guy in the basket would not be able to get Spunky Doo safely into the net. But, the one guy also confirmed, there was no room for Spunky Doo in the basket. Down came the crane with basket. Out came the guy. Back up went the empty basket.

They all looked at me. What? Oh.

"Jump!" I shouted up at Spunky Doo. "Hop! Leap!" No response. "Eject!"

Spunky Doo looked at me. What? Oh.

He looked down into the basket now positioned right under him. He looked at me. He looked at the firefighters. Who had their cameras ready. Then he lunged into the basket, face first. A cheer went up from the crowd. Unfortunately his hindquarters kind of got stuck and he didn't have any wiggle room. The crane started lowering the basket, Spunky Doo's ass end in the breeze. Cameras flashed.

As soon as the basket hit the ground, one of the guys opened the door, and Spunky Doo flopped out—but then couldn't decide whether to prance around or put his tail between his legs. So he pranced around with his tail between his legs. I thanked the firetruck crew, and they left. After a few more photographs, posed shots with Spunky Doo. The neighbors trailed away as well.

"Okay! Field trip's over!" Kessie trotted to the car, ball in mouth, Chum behind her, ditto. Hunk and Little Miss, and Spunky Doo, of course, and—wait a minute, where was Snookums?

"Snookums!" I called out. No Snookums. I called again,

"Snookums!" Then just before panic took over, I saw the tall grass move in the distance. Had to be her. "Snookums!" The grass moved again. Not much further from the first place. Was she hurt? "Snookums" I started running toward the moving grass. Suddenly it dawned on me. She was trying to bring the rabbit with her. Eew.

"Leave it!" The grass continued to move. "Drop it!" Still moved. "Let go!" By now, I had reached her. She was insistent. She would not leave the rabbit. I was insistent. I would not touch it.

The others came to see what the problem was. Hunk was the first to understand. He walked over to Snookums and before I knew it, took a bite. I heard the soft crunch of cartilage. He gave the rabbit's ear to Snookums. Little Miss was impressed. Snookums was delighted, and ready to come home.

Or not. Not in the car. No way. I have to admit, I empathized with her: motion sickness is not pleasant. This time, Chum resolved the situation. He gently picked her up, rabbit ear flopping—okay, and a little bit dripping—from her mouth. He set her gently into the front passenger seat and climbed in after her.

We dropped off Hunk and Spunky Doo with no problem, but Little Miss's person was home. She peered in at the passenger side then drew back quickly as Snookums put her little front paws on the window, barely reaching, to proudly show the somewhat unidentifiable object in her mouth, blood and whatever smeared on her—well, smeared on her.

"She got into some strawberry syrup and—"

Big Miss waited.

"Some beige pudding," I finished lamely.

OUR NEXT TRIP WAS to the beach. Fewer trees. No rabbits. It was a longer drive, though, so it was a whole day thing. No problem, said

Hunk's guy. Okay, said Big Miss, a little cautiously. Sure, said Spunky Doo's people—please. And Chum? He had gone home on his own after the field trip, but I'd remembered his number.

"Oh, he'd *love* to go to the beach with you! I'll get his beach ball out." His beach ball? Turns out it was a severely waterlogged rubber ball. Essentially a sponge ball. Chum was waiting at the door, his beach ball in his mouth, clearly understanding he was GOING TO THE WATER!! Of course. He was part lab.

Little Miss was also waiting at the door. In a bikini. Oh my god. It was an itsy bitsy, teeny weeny bikini. A yellow, polka dot bikini.

Hunk pretended not to notice. As did Chum. Spunky Doo wouldn't have noticed in any case. And Kessie didn't really care what other people wore. She had a bright green tennis ball in her mouth. And Snookums—Snookums threw up. I pulled over and with Little Miss' permission, and I suspect, her approval, took off her bikini and used it to clean up Snookum's throw-up.

Half an hour later, we arrived. I parked the car and let the dogs out. Yippee!! Woohoo! That was me, this time. I love sun, sand, and sea. Again, Kessie knew what she wanted. She'd been here before. She put her ball in my hand, got ready, then tore off down the runway of hard packed sand by the water's edge, racing after her ball. Sheer bliss.

Chum put his beach ball down at my feet, then looked expectantly out to the water. Of course! I threw it out as far as I could. He heard the plop, noted its position, then threw himself into the waves after it.

This was Snookums' first time at the beach. What would she do? Turned out she was fascinated by the water's edge. She toddled along the edge, beside me, as I walked along on the firm part. Splish, splash, plunk, plunk. She was very focused. On what, exactly, I wondered. Shiny grains of sand, perhaps? Rotten bits of fish?

Spunky Doo was running ahead and back, barking at the waves. Little Miss was walking on the other side of me, careful not to get her tootsies wet, lifting them higher than was really necessary. And Hunk. Hunk was a surprise. I don't think dobermans are known for their swimming ability. And suddenly he was out there, howling, and yipping, and squealing, and splashing at the surface with his huge paws, having the time of his life, and gulping water, and—oh my god, was he drowning? I looked at Chum, who, as part lab, was our designated Lifeguard. Until this moment, he had been repeatedly plowing through the waves with masterful and determined strokes after his soggy and increasingly forlorn beach ball. But upon hearing Hunk, he stopped, looked, and listened. And then resumed plowing through the waves with masterful and determined strokes. After his soggy and increasingly forlorn beach ball. Okay then. Little Miss had also looked to Chum. She understood he was not concerned, but she wasn't entirely convinced. She kept her eye on Hunk as she walked beside me.

Apparently Spunky Doo didn't get the memo. He dove into the water after Hunk. Whether he intended to rescue him or just join in the goofiness, we'll never know. We do know that once Spunky Doo reached Hunk, the rescue situation had to be reassessed. Again Chum stopped, looked, and listened. I looked attentively at Chum. As did Little Miss. Even Snookums paused. (Kessie used the moment to put her ball securely into my hand.) But by then Hunk had extricated himself from Spunky Doo and had struggled ashore, muttering. (Dumb ass dog, no doubt.)

Okay, it was definitely time for ice cream. We headed to the ice cream place down the beach a bit. I loved it, because they gave tasters—little plastic spoons with a dollop of whatever flavor you wanted to try before deciding which one you really wanted.

One Mint ice cream cone for Kessie, please. And Snookums liked

Butter Pecan. Though she leaves all the pecan bits. First time that happened, I thought she'd lost all of her puppy teeth at once.

Chum, what would you like? I asked for a taster of Very Cherry. No. Of course not, what was I thinking. Not Hawaiian Pineapple or Tangerine Orange either. Ah. I asked for a taster of Peanut Butter Swirl. Bingo. One Peanut Butter Swirl, please.

Little Miss, let me see...French Vanilla? Yes, got it in one! She delicately licked the spoon clean then politely waited for her cone.

Hunk...Tiger Tail Licorice? Oddly enough, yes, he liked it. 'Course, he also liked the little plastic spoon. Double scoop of that one, please. Better have lots of coating for that spoon.

Spunky Doo, what do you want? Amaretto, Praline Delight, Peachy Keen, Triple Chocolate Brownie Fudge—woof. No, sorry, you can't have that one—dogs can't have chocolate. Terrific Toffee, Candy Floss, Espresso Express—woof. I looked at him. I looked at the mile long beach. What the hell, if not now, when? Okay, one small cone of Espresso Express for Spunky Doo.

I ordered the Triple Chocolate Brownie Fudge for myself. Spunky Doo stared at me. Because I can, I told him.

The neat thing about having ice cream cones at the beach, if you're a dog, is that they can be stuck into the sand for easy consumption. And the water nearby makes for easy clean up. Unnecessary this time, however, as Snookums went around and took care of everyone's ice cream face.

We started to head back. Actually, Spunky Doo had already headed back, returned, headed back again, and returned again. When he started out a third time, Hunk accidentally stretched out his foreleg and Spunky Doo went flying. I saw him grin. Hunk, I mean. Though Spunky Doo was probably also grinning.

After a little bit, Snookums got in front of me and lifted her cute little pink paw. Carry me, I'm tired, I'm just a little baby. I picked her up, eight pounds now, and put her in her snuggly thing, where, much as she tried, she couldn't keep her eyes open.

Good idea, I thought. I headed to a shaded spot, and sat down. Almost immediately Hunk, Little Miss, and Chum dug holes to get to the cool sand, then curled up in them. Spunky Doo also dug a hole—and curled up beside it. I got comfy too. Kessie was curled up on my left, with her ball—*and* Chum's beach ball—how did that happen? And Snookums was still nestled in her snuggly thing on my right, fast asleep, wagging her tail as she dreamt. How sweet is that?

After a while, I woke up. What? I hadn't intended to fall asleep! I quickly counted the dogs—one, two, three, four, five, six, whew! Wait a minute—seven, eight, nine—what the—*fourteen* dogs were curled up and mostly asleep all around me. Snookums was awake and giggling at me from ear to ear. Aha! *She's* the one responsible for this! Probably invited every passing dog to come join us.

As she then demonstrated. The largest german shepherd I'd ever seen came our way. I snuck a look at Hunk. He was still asleep. Good. Snookums toddled over to the shepherd, all happy, and did her thing: she squiggled into a sort of log roll, ending up belly up under the dog's jaws. At first I was dismayed when I saw that this so-called submission behavior was her norm. But then I realized it was just her way of getting all the competitive stuff out of the way as quickly as possible—yes, yes, you can be the alpha dog, I'm a happy little beta, now LET'S PLAY!!

The shepherd didn't play. It opened its mouth. My, what big teeth you have. Hunk was still asleep. *Not* good. Then the shepherd, unbelievably, put his jaws around Snookums' whole head. Snookums' whole head was in his mouth. What to do?

I took my cue from her. She didn't seem to mind. Maybe it was a sign of affection. After all, he wasn't biting down. And if she was really afraid, she'd have run to me and flown into my open arms.

Literally. Once I wasn't expecting it—she had been afraid of a garbage can—and I wasn't ready. She thumped into my chest and I had to scramble to catch her as she tumbled down. But she wasn't running. She squiggled a bit more, then reached out a paw, a cute little baby paw, to touch the shepherd's mouth. He licked her. My, what a big tongue you have. She giggled. Then he decided to lay down beside her. Okay then. But he wasn't going to fit into the car, I told her.

OUR NEXT OUTING WAS to the toy store. The one that lets you bring your dogs inside. With the understanding that you'll keep your dog leashed, I know, but trust me, keeping all six leashed would have been—worse.

So we went in after I made sure they understood they could each buy one thing. *One* thing, got it? Okay.

This was Snookums' first time, and she was a little afraid, so I had to go with her to pick out her toy. I set her down, and she toddled up and down the aisles, looking back to make sure I was still with her, to make sure she was still with me. We went right through the stuffed toys aisle, and through the treats aisle, past the grooming aids, and the fashion accessories to—the cat section? There she discovered a bin full of squeaky mouse toys. She didn't just stick her head in and get one. Of course not. She jumped right into the bin. All nine pounds of her. Once in, she pounced—*squeak!*—and pounced again—*squeak!* She giggled at me. And pounced again—*squeak!* I reached down and picked her up, one moist squeaky mouse in her mouth. She burrowed into her snuggly thing, completely disappearing. *Squeak!* Okay, one down, five to go.

We found Hunk and Little Miss at the collar and leash display, sitting politely, though with controlled interest, waiting for me to get what they had their eyes on. They couldn't reach—well, they could, but they weren't going to. Good dogs. I moved my hand—*squeak!*—from one item to the next until I got a bark. From Little Miss. At the thick black leather studded collar. Okaaay. A few seconds later, Hunk barked. I had my hand on the pink rhinestone encrusted collar. Hm. Either they're engaged or they're experimenting with cross-dressing. Then again, far be it for me to our stupid gender categories on dogs.

Chum came trotting around the corner, a smallish basketball in his mouth. Of course. He's a ball dog. Or maybe he'd just watched Air Bud a lot.

Kessie found us next, dragging something, with great effort, ass end in the air. I couldn't see what—ah—a 100-pack of bright fluorescent green tennis balls.

Okay, off to the checkout. We stood in line. *Squeak!* The cashier smiled, as she dealt with the customer ahead of us. *Squeak!* She smiled again and snuck a glance at the lump in the snuggly thing that was Snookums. Then it was our turn.

"Hi, how are—" *Squeak!* "What have you got in there?" She babytalked to Snookums. "Let me see," she coaxed, "what have you got?" *Squeak!* She gently pulled back a corner of the snuggly. A teeny little nose appeared. Then a teeny little muzzle appeared, jaws clamped tight. "Have you got a mouse?" Snookums shook her head back and forth, a tail hanging out of her mouth.

"Do you need me to get the tag for you?" I asked.

She looked at our line-up. "It's only a buck. Don't worry about it."

"Okay, thanks." I reached down then to get Kessie's bag of tennis balls. She wouldn't let go. Silly me. What was I thinking? I picked her up then, still holding on to her bag of tennis balls, and set her on the conveyor belt. She stood there, the bag as big as her. The cashier activated the belt. Surf city, here we come! She scanned the tag as Kess went by.

Chum was next in line. He put his paws up, set his basketball carefully onto the belt, and gently rolled it toward the cashier with his nose. Okay, he *had* watched Air Bud. A lot.

Hunk and Little Miss walked past next, each with the other's collar—or not. They graciously allowed me to take the collars, get them scanned, then give them back.

Then we heard a crash over in the stuffed toy section. Spunky Doo—where was Spunky Doo? Dare I call him? And hear half a dozen more crashes as he came racing to answer my call? No, give him another couple seconds. We heard another crash, a little closer. That made just two, please note. Then we saw him bounding around the corner and—what the—? He was wearing his toy. A giant purple furry octopus was somehow wrapped around his neck, its garish head appearing to rise out of his own, making him look like some ridiculous two-headed cartoon alien. *And* he had a huge caveman rawhide bone in his mouth. Must've been three feet across. That was two things. But okay. The brontosaurus bone was probably going to save a dining room set. He got in line with us at the checkout, relieved to have made it in time. With no idea how ridiculous he looked. Then again, given the grin on his face, he was probably perfectly aware of how ridiculous he looked.

Seeing that it was his turn, he eagerly stepped forward. Whack! The brontosaurus bone wouldn't fit. Spunky Doo backed up and stepped forward again. Whack! Oddly enough, it still wouldn't fit. He backed up and stepped forward a third time. Whack! (Then again, about that dining room set…) Hunk, until now sitting patiently beside Little Miss on the other side of the checkout, lay down. This was going to take some time.

"If we don't help him, how many more times do you think he'll do that?" The cashier asked, barely concealing her laughter. Good question.

Spunky Doo backed up again. "No, wait!" I reached out my hand. He looked at it curiously, then he looked up at me, then back down at my hand, the octopus head bobbing up and down as he did so. What? Hunk groaned.

"Give. Let Go. Release." No response. "Look, it won't fit sideways, give it to me, and I'll carry it through for you, the other way." Oh. Why didn't you say that?

So we got Spunky Doo through the checkout and then headed out to my car. Once there, everyone looked pointedly at Spunky Doo's brontosaurus bone, then at the car, then at the bone, then at me. Right. Someone's liable to get knocked out. Probably me. I opened the trunk and put the bone inside. Spunky Doo jumped in after it, his purple octopus head bobbing up and down. No—okay, yeah—no, get in the back seat, you.

OUR LAST OUTING AS a group was to the dog show. 'Course, I didn't know it was our last group outing. Then again, I didn't know dogs shouldn't be taken to dog shows. Go figure.

The show was held at the city's huge arena. Inside, different areas of the arena were marked off for different shows or competitions or whatever. The first one we came to was the puppy agility course. You know the course I'm talking about: it has various obstacles the dogs have to jump over, climb through, walk across, run around, and so on. We all settled into the bleachers to watch the first group of puppies. Five of them were let loose at the starting line and given various encouragements to more or less head off in the right direction.

One simply had no idea. It sat down. Two scampered off together toward the first obstacle, but then got tangled up before they got there. They snarled and snapped at each other—they couldn't wait to be big dogs. Which would probably happen next week. The fourth puppy stopped to piddle. Then forgot what it was supposed to be doing. The fifth one ran *into* the obstacle. Fell down, laughed. The sixth little one made it to the obstacle, and even made it over, but was then so delighted with itself it had to run over to—us. See what I did? Did you see? I climbed over it! I did! Unfortunately, leaving the course gets you disqualified. However, if you're not formally entered in the first place... We all congratulated Snookums. Yes, we did see! We know! And not only did you climb over the obstacle, you did it with a mouse in your mouth! What a clever little puppy! Then we stuffed her into her snuggly thing and moved on to the next area.

Which was the tennis ball relay race. Two dogs race to jump on a springboard, which releases a tennis ball, which they catch, then race back with, so the next dog on their team can race down the stretch to the springboard, and so on, four dogs to a team. We settled into the bleachers to watch. Kessie leaned forward, her interest rather—intense. Suddenly I felt her gently put her ball into my hand, but before I could tell her this was not the time nor place, she shot off the bleachers, and in an amazing feat of speed, timing, and coordination, intercepted the tennis ball in mid-fire and flew back to her spot in the bleachers. Leaving the border collie—the breed reputed to be the genius of the species, I might point out—staring dumbly at the hole, waiting for the ball to pop out. Kessie put her newly acquired ball into my hand. I looked around innocently as I slipped it into Snookums' snuggly—*squeak!* Then Kess shot off the bleachers again. I put the second ball into the snuggly—*squeak!*—then grabbed her just as she crouched for her third launch, and moved us all quickly to the next area.

It was the show portion of the show. We were in time for the poodle class. First one poodle, then another, strutted down the runway, all fluffed and shaved and manicured and be-ribboned. Cameras flashed. Hunk started howling. His equivalent to a wolf whistle, I guess. 'Cuz it distracted Contestant #3. Contestant #4 actually 'lost her carriage'—or whatever the correct dog show phrase is for 'tripped'. Then Contestant #5 howled—at Little Miss. Well. Hunk was confused. He didn't know poodles came in male. Or that male dogs did the show thing. (Though, of course, if any male dog did, it would be a male poodle.) So he didn't know whether he wanted to howl at the next contestant or attack the previous one. His next howl had a growl at the end. Well, that got Contestant #6 all excited. She hit the floor, paws down, rump up, in the classic invitation-to-play posture. Well, okay, the classic invitation to—her rump was *facing* Hunk.

Then Contestant #7 was announced.

"No, sorry," the announcer stumbled to correct himself, "there doesn't seem to be a—"

I don't know where she got the bonnet from, let alone who helped her put it on. No, wait. Yes I do. It was on backwards. But there she was. Too sexy for Milan, too sexy for Milan, and as she did her little turn on the catwalk, Hunk lost it. He let out a howl as he flew off the bleachers straight to Little Miss. Cameras flashed. They made the third page, local news. Same day as Spunky Doo.

2

JOCKO

When they say there's no such thing as bad publicity, they're right. I had thought that my dog walking days would be over, but, in fact, my business seemed to expand. Some calls were for dog walking, but I also got can I take their dog to the groomer, can I take their dog for the weekend, can I take their dog.

And one day I got, "Jocko won't leave the property."

Okay. Usually this is a good thing.

"He won't get into my truck."

And…

"The Fosters told me what you did with Spunky Doo—"

What? What did I do with Spunky Doo?

"—so I thought maybe you could help Jocko."

"Oh. I thought you were calling about my dog walking services."

"No, they said you were a dog therapist or something."

"They did?" They didn't tell me they still had their dining room set.

"Yeah."

"Okay." Cool.

So I asked for his address. He didn't really have an address. He said he lived on five acres of bush outside of town. I got directions.

"Kessie, Snookums, we're going into the bush!" I called to them.

Kess came running. Can I bring my ball?

I looked at her, one of her five current tennis balls stuffed in her mouth. That really wasn't a question, was it.

Snookums was now ten pounds and almost six months old. She had stopped throwing up in the car, but hadn't quite realized it. Or still remembered the nausea. Either way, she remained a little reluctant to travel.

"There will be creatures to kill," I told her.

All right then. She grinned. And raised her little baby paw to be picked up and carried into the car. She could walk out to the car by herself, of course, and even jump in, but she was still playing up the baby thing for all it was worth. I didn't mind a bit.

HALF AN HOUR LATER, we pulled into a dirt driveway. Well, more like across it, since there wasn't quite enough room behind the monster truck that was parked there. There were many things about the property that would have upset the Neighborhood Association. Had there been one. What there was, I noted, was an elderly gentleman across the way sitting on a chair on his porch. Clearly whatever happened at Jocko's place was better than tv.

I nodded to him as I got out of the car. He nodded back. Wondering what today's show was going to be all about.

Kessie and Snookums trotted beside me toward the house, both knowing better than to go the other way toward the road. Snookums ran ahead to say hi to Jocko, a bulldog boxer mix, by the look of him, with a gorgeous brown coat tiger-streaked with gold. He was sitting on the driveway beside the porch, tension strung through his body, anxiety sharpening his face—and one of those electric fence collars around his neck. Ah.

"You're Brett?" The man who came out of the house had a Grizzly-Adams-gone-to-beer thing going.

"Yes, you're—"

"I'm Bud."

Of course you are.

"So..."

"Jocko kept taking off into the bush, sometimes it'd be days before he came back..."

And you never went looking for him? If Kess or Snookums disappeared for ten minutes, I'd be freaking. Speaking of which, Kess was beside me, waiting patiently for me to throw her ball into the bush, and Snookums was on her back, squiggling into Jocko, squiggling under Jocko, pawing up at his muzzle. His tail was thumping, and he was nuzzling her neck. Then he stood up, the better to nuzzle other parts of her.

"...so I got one of them electric fences. I buried the wire around the perimeter," he gestured grandly, but vaguely, out toward the bush around us, "put the collar on him, and turned it on."

I looked out. "Where are the flags?"

"What flags?"

"The flags you were supposed to put along where you buried the wire."

"I buried the wire along the property line," he said. As if I was an idiot for thinking he might do otherwise.

"Yeah, but I have no idea where your property line is—what makes you think Jocko knows? You were supposed to walk him along—didn't you read the instructions that came with the fence?"

Of course not. Real men don't read instructions.

"He figured it out," he dismissed my suggestions as 'babying' the dog. Heaven forbid.

"Well, he didn't quite. Did he. He's not leaving the property even when you want him to."

"Yeah, that's why I called you."

Right. So it was *my* problem.

"Okay, so after you buried the wire, put the collar on him, turned it on—then what happened?" I asked. Knowing full well.

"Well, I guess he got zapped a couple times," he said in a serves-him-right voice, "but now when I call him to get into the truck, he won't come."

I went to Jocko to say hello. Snookums rolled onto her feet, smiling, and Jocko sat back down, resuming his tense vigilance.

"Hey, Jocko, how are you?" I held out my hand under his nose, palm up, for him to smell. Then I scratched him behind his ears, then crouched and ran my hands along his sides. "Are you being a good dog?" His tail thumped. Snookums' wagged. "I'll bet you are! I'll bet you're a very good dog." He gave me a few licks. Snookums gave me a few licks. Snookums gave Jocko a few licks. I gave Jocko, and Snookums, a treat from my pocket, which was always full. Unless I happened to throw my jacket onto the floor, in which case the pocket would be mysteriously empty next time I checked.

"Okay," I half-turned to Bud, "so when he heard the beep—"

"What beep?"

I reached down to Jocko's collar—he flinched. Then he stood up. Hm.

"It's okay," I crooned to him, "let me see..." I scratched his ears again then gently eased the collar off. There were two raw, red spots where the contact prongs had been.

"You haven't been taking this off at night?" I asked Bud angrily. A shock on raw, exposed skin would hurt like hell, I thought.

The man just stared.

"Do you have some Polysporin or something—to put on these sores?"

He grunted and went into the house. I slipped the collar into my pocket. No way was it ever going on Jocko again. Not if I could help it. The man came back out, and handed me a tube of antibiotic cream. Apparently, he was not about to play nurse.

I bent down to Jocko. "It's okay," I said, as I uncapped the tube. "Sit. That's a good dog. Stay." I doubted he'd been taught any of those words, the basics of what would enable him and his person to communicate, but he was smart enough to figure out what I was doing. My tone told him. I was helping him. That was all he needed to know.

"It's okay," I repeated. Snookums told him the same thing. Even Kessie came over. "It's okay, that's a good dog, good Jocko..." I continued to croon to him as I dabbed some of the cream on each of his sore spots.

Then I stood up and handed the tube back to Bud.

"You were supposed to stick the flags along the line where you buried the wire. So he'd know where the line was. Then whenever he got near the line, and he heard the beep—"

"I told you I never heard a beep."

"No, the frequency is beyond your range of hearing. But Jocko would—" Jeezus. I pulled the collar out of my pocket and examined it.

"You have it set to just correction."

He didn't know what I was talking about.

"You're supposed to start by setting it to warn him first, with a high-pitched beep, so he knows the shock is coming if he keeps going. And you're supposed to make him understand what to do when he hears the beep. How is he supposed to know that he's supposed to turn back toward the house? Maybe he's supposed to keep going. Maybe he's supposed to stand still. How is he supposed to know if you don't explain it to him?

"Once he understands where the property line is, and that he'll get zapped if he crosses it, you don't even need the fence. You can take down the flags, you can take off the collar."

If a dog understands what you want, I was tempted to add, and wants to do what you want, you wouldn't even have needed the fence. You could just call it back whenever it started to cross the line and reward it, with treats and praise and lots of snuggles, for coming back. End of story.

For some, depending on what was across the line, that might need to be stepped up a bit with a firm "NO!" or a scream, but frankly, I thought the whole electric fence thing was often just a replacement for time and effort—for love.

"Then you were supposed to identify a safe crossing spot, where the dog knew that when given a certain command, like 'Cross Over', it could cross over without getting hurt. Of course, you'd deactivate the fence, or take off the collar, for those crossovers."

He grunted.

"But you didn't do any of that. So as far as Jocko's concerned," I said, "he was just minding his own business, doing what he always does, then one day a monster came out of nowhere and bit him on the neck. And now it keeps coming out of nowhere—he can't see it, and worse, he can't smell it or hear it coming—and it keeps attacking him. For no reason. Whenever he goes," I gestured to his property. "Given that, I'm surprised he's even left the driveway."

The man looked down.

"He hasn't? He hasn't left the driveway in all this time?!"

But then why was he nervous even here on the driveway? Ah. The attacks weren't random on the driveway, so to that extent it was a safe zone. But he had tried to escape. And had gotten zapped where the line crossed the driveway.

Okay, I thought, first we get Jocko to understand about the beeps. Kessie and Snookums would be a distraction, so I headed back to my car to put them inside. Jocko flew from his spot by the porch and flung himself in front of us, blocking our path.

This guy *so* does not deserve this dog.

"Fucking dog!" He reached over and cuffed him one.

"No!" I yelled at him. At Bud. Not Jocko. And cuffed *him* one. He stared at me. Shocked.

"He was trying to protect us. From getting hurt by the monster!" I turned to Jocko, bent down, and hugged him. Kess and Snookums gathered round for reassurance. They'd been temporarily confused by my yelling "No!"

"Good dog, Jocko," I stroked him. "Yes, good Kessie and Snookums too," they crowded in for snuggles. "Such a good dog, good Jocko, thank you. Good dog." I overdid it. I had to, to cancel the asshole's reprimand. Jocko wagged his tail. He too overdid it. He'd probably never been praised before. For anything.

Asshole.

The more so because he didn't even realize that Jocko had made no attempt to protect him from the monster. Ever.

I led Jocko back to the porch.

"Do you have a leash or something?" I turned to Bud.

He went into the garage and returned with a dirty, frayed rope.

I tied one end to a porch post and wound the other around—Jocko's chest. He was trembling.

"It's okay, I'll be back in a minute," I told him, and gave him a few more ear scratches.

As soon as we approached the property line, he howled. I didn't look back, but knew he'd thrown himself forward, straining on the rope. We crossed the line. Kessie and Snookums didn't get attacked. Surely he saw that. I put them both in the front seat, then rolled down both of the back seat windows as far as they would go. It was a hot day and I'd be a while. Then I went back to Jocko to show him that I was okay.

"Okay," I turned to Bud then. "First, we're going to put the flags along the line of the property, where you buried the wire. So Jocko understands the danger isn't random."

He stared at me, dully.

"You still have the flags?"

"Yeah." He went into the garage and came out with a cardboard box full of flags.

I pulled the collar out of my pocket, set it to 'warning plus correction', slapped it on the guy's upper arm, turning the prongs to the inside tender flesh, and tightened it—all before he figured out what I was doing.

"Okay, start walking." I untied the rope from the porch, and Jocko and I started walking behind him. Jocko was reluctant, to say the least, but I continued to croon to him, telling him it was okay, and letting him lean into me as much as he wanted.

Almost immediately there was a beep. I could tell only because Jocko's ears perked. I pulled him gently toward me, toward the center of the property, where the house was, gave him a treat, told him he was a good dog, snuggled him.

"Ow!" the guy said a couple seconds later.

"Plant a flag," I said, and we walked on.

Jocko's ears perked a few meters on, I pulled him gently toward the center, gave him a treat, told him he was a good dog, snuggled him.

"Damn it!"

The guy planted another flag.

"They have to be closer together," I said. "Dogs don't connect the dots very well."

Jocko's ears perked again. I pulled him gently toward the center, gave him a treat, told him he was a good dog, snuggled him.

"Fuck!"

Three flags later, I cut out the occasional treat.

By the time we were half way around the property, I just gave praise and snuggles.

"Christ!"

And three flags after that, Jocko was pushing me toward the center as soon as he heard the beep. He got it.

That is to say, he understood that when he heard a beep, he was to move back, toward the house. But since I hadn't let him get shocked, there was no reason for him to connect the beeps to the monster. So although he'd never again get bit on the neck out of nowhere, he didn't know that. Eventually, I hoped, he'd leave the driveway to roam through the bush on the property and realize the monster was gone. Or, if he ignored the beep once, he'd realize it was still there, but only on the far side of the beeps.

"Okay," I said when we were back at the driveway, "now we just have to teach him to cross over." I bent down and snuggled Jocko, telling him what a good job he'd just done.

"And I'm telling you," Bud said, petulant and rubbing his arm, "when I call him, he doesn't come."

I turned my attention to Bud. "Okay, so what you've been doing is you go to your truck—which you usually park where it is now, right?" I pointed this out, hoping he realized then that while garage itself was on this side of the line, his truck, unless he pulled it right up to the garage, was on the other side of the line. Jocko had figured this out weeks ago. "And then you just call him."

"And he won't come!"

No shit.

"And I had the fence turned off!"

"Okay, but how would Jocko know you'd killed the monster?"

"What?"

"Never mind." Jocko obviously didn't trust the guy. I didn't blame him.

"Okay, so we need you to do something obvious and out of the ordinary to indicate to Jocko that you've killed the monster."

I thought for a moment. Having him do the Chicken Dance would make him feel silly, but having him do the Macarena would humiliate him. Back in 1995, nothing said 'I'm a woman' like the Macarena (sigh), and he was old enough to remember. And stupid enough to think that anything even remotely associated with being a woman was inferior—and therefore humiliating.

"Okay, go over the line to your truck and do the Macarena."

"What?"

"Dogs respond well to visual cues. And doing the Macarena is enough out of the ordinary, it will make an impression on him. He'll notice. He'll understand you're doing something special. Hopefully, we can make him understand that what you're doing is killing the monster."

He walked over to his truck. And just stood there.

"Go on," I said, and started humming. He just stood there.

The man across the street leaned forward in his chair.

"Stay," I said to Jocko, and went to stand beside the guy. Jocko stayed, but watched anxiously.

"Come on," I said, humming from the beginning again, and

going through the motions. Right hand out, left hand out, right hand flip over, left hand flip over. Bud followed. Right hand onto left shoulder, left hand onto right shoulder, right hand behind head, left hand behind head. Bud, so help him, followed. The man across the street was grinning. Right hand onto left hip, left hand onto right hip—Bud hesitated.

"Come on, you have to do the whole thing," I lied. Right hand onto right butt, left hand onto left butt, move hips in a circle, clap, jump and turn.

The man across the street was shaking with barely contained laughter.

Jocko stared at us.

Which was good. He was obviously seeing something totally unusual.

"Okay, Jocko, cross over," I called out to him. "Come here!"

Jocko didn't move.

"See?" The guy was disgusted.

"Oh, it's going to take more than one time for him to get it. Do it again," I said, going to sit beside Jocko. To watch.

Bud did the Macarena again. Well, he did a seriously abridged version. But what he did—hands onto shoulders, hands onto hips—"Don't forget to swivel your hips", I shouted—hip swivel, clap, jump, turn—was probably good enough. It was clearly enough to have Jocko's complete attention. And the man across the street had gone into the house, no doubt to get his wife.

"Now say 'Cross over' and call him."

"Jocko, cross over!"

Jocko didn't move. I, however, crossed over. I stood by the truck, facing Jocko, and ate a treat. (Pretended. They smelled like salmon, but they tasted like vomit. I have no idea why dogs like them so much.) (Then again—) I returned to Jocko to show him I was okay.

"Again," I called out to Bud.

Hands on shoulders, hands on hips, swivel hips, clap, jump, turn. "Cross over!"

Again I crossed over, stood by the truck, and pretended to eat a treat. Again, I returned to Jocko to show him I was okay.

"Again," I called out.

Hands on shoulders, hands on hips, swivel hips, clap, jump, turn. "Cross over!"

"Come on, Jocko, it's okay," I said. "You can 'cross over'!" I encouraged him to come with me. He stood up, quivering. He wanted to. He wanted to cross over so badly.

"Again!" I called out. We were almost there, I thought.

Hands on shoulders, hands on hips, swivel hips, clap, jump, turn. "Cross over!"

Jocko didn't. Couldn't. It suddenly occurred to me that maybe the monster attacked only dogs.

Okay, time for Kessie to help out. I headed to my car, but stopped at the line.

"Again," I said to Bud.

This time, when he said 'Cross over', I crossed over, went to my car, and got Kessie. Snookums didn't have 'Stay' and 'Come here' quite as firmly as Kessie, and I didn't want to risk confusing Jocko even more. She was sound asleep in the driver's seat anyway, having one of her little puppy naps, wagging her tail, dreaming. Of disemboweled rabbits, no doubt.

I led Kessie to Jocko.

"Sit." Kessie sat.

"Stay." Kessie stayed. And watched me walk away from her. I joined Bud on the other side of the line and was glad that the first gesture of the Macarena was an outstretched arm, which was, coincidentally the gestural command for 'Stay' that I'd taught Kessie. I had always taught both a verbal and a visual command so if, when, she started losing her hearing or her vision, she could still understand what I wanted. If it came to needing to be told what I wanted.

As soon as we clapped and jumped, I crouched with my arms wide open. "Okay, come here!" I said enthusiastically. Kessie flew from her spot into my arms. Jocko took note. Kessie had not been attacked. The Macarena killed the monster!

I led her back to Jocko.

"Sit. Stay."

I left her again, crossed the line to Bud, and we did the Macarena one more time. To the delight of the small crowd that had gathered across the street.

This time, as soon as I'd clapped and jumped, Jocko sprang up, flew across the line, ran straight past me, and leapt clear through the open window into my car.

HE SETTLED INTO OUR household quite nicely that evening: Kessie didn't mind his presence, since he left her ball alone, and as far as Snookums was concerned, the more the merrier. She helped me prepare the guest bed—I'd bought a large doggy bed a while ago for our overnight guests, onto which I now bunched up a freshly laundered blanket—then brought a little squeaky mouse from her bowlful in the bedroom and set it on top of the blanket.

NEXT AFTERNOON I FOUND Chum sitting beside the car as usual. As far as he was concerned, he'd discovered the bus stop for the free shuttle service to and from the dog park, the field, and the beach. So after my morning pot of tea, I bundled Kessie, Snookums, Chum, and Jocko into the car and we headed to the dog park.

That was when I realized Jocko would be better off living with someone else.

Kess, Snookums, and Chum jumped out, free at last, thank god we're free at last, but when Jocko got out, he took one look out at the open green expanse and leaned into me, quivering. It was another minefield.

I thought about just putting him back into the car to wait while the rest of us had our romp, but I knew he'd watch our every step with great anxiety until he could no longer see us—and then what? I didn't want to put him through that.

So we went back home, I put him inside the house, and then took the other three back to the park for a shortish romp.

When we returned, I started making phone calls. Two hours later, Jocko and I drove to 4299 LaSalle Drive. I knocked on the door of Apartment #9. Normally, I don't think people who live in apartments should have big dogs. Especially if they don't take them for runs every day. But in this case, the front 'yard' filled with chipped stone and a neighbourhood with nothing but sidewalks and pavement as far as the eye could see—for Jocko, it was safety, security, peace of mind.

ALICIA CALLED ME A week later. She had discovered that several people in her neighborhood took their dogs to the nearby school late at night. Its playground was the best they could do for a dog park. It was fenced, which made it safe for the dogs to be off-leash, but it was literally a concrete jungle—not a blade of grass in sight.

Jocko loved it.

She'd also discovered something else.

"I'm so glad you told me what he'd been through," she said. "We happened to be at a crosswalk for the blind one day. He heard the beep and froze. Refused to cross. Blocked the way and wouldn't let me cross either."

"That's good!" I said, genuinely pleased.

"No, he was rigid with fear!"

"Well, yeah, he probably had a bit of a post-traumatic flashback," I said, "but he kept his head and—he blocked your way. That's the good part. He obviously cares for you. Very much."

"Yeah," she said after a few seconds. I could hear the smile in her voice and knew, I just knew, that he had that gorgeous head in her lap, and that she was scratching his ears.

"The feeling is mutual," she added, "and we won't ever be crossing at Main and Third again. Or at any of the other beeping crosswalks. I called the City and found out where every single one of them is."

I smiled, and we hung up a few seconds later.

Then I sat there, thinking about happy ever after endings. Jocko certainly wouldn't've stepped in front of Bud. I wondered if he would've stepped behind him, then pushed him into the intersection. I know I would've.

3

CARSON

The following week, I received another call.

"Carson won't come into the house."

Hm.

"Carson is a dog?" Just making sure.

AS I PULLED UP to the house, I saw Carson lying in the front yard, as far from the house as the long rope she was attached to would allow. She was a cute little spaniel.

Or would be if I could make the pain in her eyes go away. Even from a distance, I could see something was seriously wrong. Surely they'd taken her to the vet, I told myself as I walked up the patio stone path to—it hit me. A wave of stench. Of cigarette and perfume. So strong, I immediately started getting a—ah. Carson, her sense of smell being 10 to 100 *thousand* times better than mine, because she has *220* million olfactory receptors, whereas I have a measly 5 million, must have the *worst* headache. She probably feels like her skull is about to implode. Or has been fracturing apart in a never-ending slow-motion tectonic— Or maybe she feels like someone's been pounding away— I massaged my temple.

And if the smell was in her luxurious black-and-white coat, as I'm sure it must be, she wouldn't've been unable to get away from it all this time. Weeks, apparently. I'll bet she wants to die.

I hesitated, then realized that my clothes probably already stink, even from ten feet away, so I was going to have to wash them. When I was a dj, and smoking was still allowed in public buildings, I had designated dj clothes that would never come into the house; I'd take them off outside my house, dump them in a waiting pail of soapy water to soak overnight, then rinse them and hang them up to dry, outside, leaving them there until next gig.

I approached the forlorn little dog, crooning. "Hey, Carson, how are you?" I said every so softly, crouching down and reaching into my pocket for a treat. She looked up at me, head throbbing. Couldn't even bother to get up. Probably felt nauseous at the thought of a treat. I reached out my hand—she lifted her head and pressed it against my palm. I reached out with my other hand and cupped her head. She wagged her tail, ever so slightly. I thought about where her temples might be.

The front door slammed. I winced. Carson winced.

"Are you Brett?"

"Yes," I stood up.

The man came toward me, hand outstretched.

He smelled, yes, but—a woman followed, cigarette in one hand and, I swear, atomizer in the other.

"Randy, is this the woman you talked about?" Hair doesn't come in yellow, I thought to myself. And lips don't come in scarlet.

"Yeah, hon, this is Brett."

I backed away from her. And there was no way I was going into the house.

"Carson has a headache," I said. "And so do I. From your cigarette smoke and your perfume."

They didn't seem to understand.

"When did Carson start refusing to go inside?" I asked.

"Right after Sherry moved in. A couple weeks ago. We thought Carson was just a bit jealous, you know, and would get over it," he smiled at Sherry. Who sidled up to him. "But you think she has a headache?"

"I think her head is throbbing so hard—*my* head is throbbing," I reached up to my temple again, "and her sense of smell is a thousand times stronger, *ten* thousand times stronger, possibly a *hundred* thousand times stronger, than mine. So what do you think?"

They looked at each other in confusion.

"Why do you think all that no-smoking and fragrance-free legislation was passed? Simply because a bunch of people didn't *approve*?"

"Tell you what—" I was so eager to get away, I didn't really think this through. "I'll take Carson and give her a bath—the smoke and perfume is in her coat, she's probably had the migraine of all migraines since you moved in," I barely glanced at Sherry. I wanted to kill her. She was causing me a lot of pain.

"You take the drapery to the drycleaners, shampoo the furniture and the carpets, wipe down the ceiling and walls and ... everything, with something strong, but unscented, leave all the windows open for a week—then call me."

"Oh," I added, in case they didn't get it, "and you'll either have to give up smoking and stop wearing that gawd-awful perfume or move out."

I untied Carson's rope and led her to my car. She came willingly. Shit. This was the part I didn't think through. Once I let Carson into my car, I was going to have to shampoo the car. Thoroughly. When I drove home from my dj gigs, I wore a plastic raincoat. Damn it. Well, there was no way I was leaving her here.

"Do you have any large plastic garbage bags?" I turned back to the man.

"Sure. Hang on."

He went back into his house, and came out with a box. I pulled out the first five and handed them to him, then kept the sixth one, the one that had been so inside the box it couldn't possibly be contaminated. I hoped.

I tore a hole out the top. Not as easy as it sounds, by the way. Then I put it over poor little Carson like a poncho, wrapped the end under her bottom, and set her carefully on the back seat. I got in, 'forgot' to wave, then backed out of the driveway.

Carson tore her way out of the plastic bag in three seconds.

And—this was the other part I didn't think through. No way I was taking her inside *my* house. To give her a bath in my tub. I didn't want to be taking *my* drapery to the cleaners and shampooing all of *my* furniture and carpets. I had an outdoor hose, but my experience was that most dogs didn't like being sprayed with a hose. Spunky Doo excepted. And I didn't have one of those little wading pools. Oh well, the beach it is, then.

Problem was, now I had to go home and get Snookums and Kessie. Couldn't go to the beach without them. But they wouldn't know, you're saying. Oh listen to yourself. Of course they'd know. They'd smell it on me. Once I got the smoke and perfume out of my clothes. Which I could do at the beach. Good thing it was a hot and sunny day. Okay, so I'd just have to give Snookums and Kessie a bath as well.

I thought about the car on my way home to get Kessie and Snookums. And Chum. How he knew we were going to the beach, I'll never know, but there he was, sitting at my driveway, looking up the road, waiting for me. His beach ball in his mouth.

So he'd had to have a bath as well. I pulled out my phone. In for a penny…

"Impromptu trip to the beach, bath included, can Spunky Doo come?"

"Of course. And for the record? The answer's always yes. Whenever, for whatever. I'll have a key made for you."

"Impromptu trip to the beach, bath included, can Hunk come?"

"Um…yeah, sure. He's moping around, I don't know what's wrong with him."

"He misses Little Miss," I said, again. Ever since the dog show fiasco, Little Miss' person had refused to let her come with us, even though I'd assured her that Hunk had been neutered. Every time I picked him up, Hunk moaned when I turned left at the critical intersection instead of right. "Did you call her? Little Miss' person?"

"Um, no, I forgot."

Asshole.

THEY ALL KEPT THEIR distance from Carson. Kess firmly pressed herself into my lap, Snookums crowded Chum on the front passenger seat, which she did in any case, and Spunky Doo leaned into Hunk, who, oddly enough, didn't protest, at the other end of the back seat. Just as well. I suspect Carson wasn't in the mood to be social.

Maybe I could find a carwash service close to the beach. Arrange for someone to follow me to the beach, take my car back, shampoo it, three times, then bring it back to the beach.

Or I could just sell it. My head had *really* started to throb. Despite having turned the fan on to high and opened all of the windows. I should've taken an extra-strength Ibuprofen or something.

I pulled into the parking lot at the pet store and once inside, headed straight to the shampoo aisle. I found something that was both unscented and biodegradable. Grabbed a bottle. Changed my mind. Grabbed the gallon jug. Paid without a word, fingers to my temple.

As I exited the store, I saw Kessie, Hunk, and Chum sitting in a circle on the pavement some distance from my car. Shit! Where was Snookums? Frantic, I scanned the entire parking lot as I broke into a run. No Snookums. Okay, maybe she was still in the car. How did Kessie get out without breaking her leg? And where was Spunky Doo? I couldn't see him in the car or anywhere in the parking lot.

As I approached, Kessie and Chum parted a little. Snookums was barricaded inside their circle. As was Spunky Doo. Who was being repeatedly nudged, perhaps even nipped, by Hunk. Maybe Spunky Doo was supposed to have been part of the protective perimeter. It was unclear to me. And probably to him as well.

I watched in disbelief then as Chum, closest to the passenger door, crouched down a bit. Kessie leapfrogged over him back in through the window. Snookums followed.

"Good dogs," I hugged Chum and Hunk when I got to them. "Such good dogs," I put my arms around each of them. I opened the front door for Chum, and the back door for Hunk and Spunky Doo. Carson was, as expected, still lying listless in the corner of the back seat.

AS LUCK WOULD HAVE it, I passed the high school on the way to the beach, and they were having a carwash. My first clue was the music. I could hear it from a block away. The original Rose Royce. Seriously?

I passed half a dozen of them dancing at the edge of the road, waving huge signs—'CAR WASH $10'.

They were clearly having a good time. A very good time. Perfect.

I pulled in, nodded to the motley, and wet, crew at the road, then stopped near the small crowd of teenagers closer to the building, surrounded by pails, rags, sponges, washing—more or less—a silver minivan. There was another small crowd a little further away working on a black SUV.

"Hey, how's it going?" I said. As soon as they saw my carful of dogs, the two small crowds converged into a large crowd. The silver minivan was momentarily forgotten. As was the black SUV. Two kids reached in to pet Chum. Kessie scampered over and put her tennis ball into the hand of one of them. Ever hopeful.

"No," I said, reaching to retrieve the ball. "Soon."

Two others at my side cooed at Snookums, who had traded places with Kessie and so was now in my lap. She wagged her tail.

Then Spunky Doo wriggled his way out the window—and went immediately to the group that was dancing. He joined in. The kids were delighted.

I quickly got out of the car. "Spunky Doo!" He was too close to the road. Fortunately, three of the kids danced him back to me, giggling all the way. Especially the one trying to teach him a bit of ballet.

"So," I said to the crowd-at-large. "Do you have stuff to do the interiors as well? Like real upholstery shampoo things?"

"No, we just have rags, pails, and shit," a tall young man said.

"Do you need your interior done?" A big and blonde young woman stepped forward, then stopped. Her nose twitched. "What *is* that smell?"

"Cigarette smoke and—"

"Chanel No. 5," someone else identified it. "I thought they outlawed that stuff."

"Apparently not," I said, then briefly told them about rescuing Carson from the world's worst headache and then having the world's second worst headache myself.

"They have those upholstery things at the grocery store," another young woman, compact and freckled, offered, nodding across the street. "You could rent one."

I glanced across the street. "Tell you what," I said to them. "A hundred bucks if one of *you* goes over and rents one, and a couple others follow me to the beach, to drive back my car, then you shampoo it, many many times, then deliver it back to me at the beach when it's done."

They conferred among themselves.

"We've got a better idea," one of them said. A bunch of them proceeded to heft Spunky Doo back in through the window, then stood aside as the freckled girl half-climbed half-dove in after him.

"Cool." I smiled. Oh to be fifteen. Sixteen. I hoped. With a valid driver's licence.

"SO," SHE SAID, HAVING found herself nose to nose with Hunk, a doberman, "Is he friendly?"

I grinned as I turned out of the parking lot. "Do you still have both arms?"

She laughed. "Hey you," she addressed Hunk. "You're a big—guy?"

I nodded. Hunk didn't respond. I really needed to resolve the Little Miss problem.

A FEW MINUTES LATER, we pulled into the parking lot at the beach. I let the dogs out (yes, that was me), grabbed my gallon jug of shampoo, then turned to Sam, the freckled young woman.

"Two hours?" I asked, handing her my car keys.

"Should be long enough."

"And not a trace of smell. Or I'll just have to do this all over again."

"You got it." She looked at Carson, huddled at my feet, the only one not already splish splashing at the water. "Poor thing."

ONCE I ASSURED MYSELF that we had the beach to ourselves, and everyone was safe doing their thing, I turned to Carson. She'd be first to get a bath. And again the last. At least. I took off her collar, washed it, then put it in my pocket. Might just buy her a new one. Then I picked her up and walked to the water. I waded in, then knelt and set her down. She was very cooperative. Or so depressed she didn't care what anyone did to her. Wet, lather, rinse. Repeat. I ran my fingers through her coat, working the shampoo right into her skin. I was thorough. Wet, lather, rinse. And repeat again. She shook herself, then walked out of the water, and despondently lay down in the sand.

Chum was next. He'd been in the front seat and so hopefully the smoke and perfume hadn't permeated his coat that much, but he had the thickest coat of the bunch. Clearly he'd been given baths at the beach before. He set his waterlogged beach ball on the sand, beside Carson—sweet—then stood still in the shallow water as I lathered him. He was, of course, already wet. I then retrieved his ball and threw it out as far as I could. He swam after it. And now he was rinsed.

Kessie's turn. Wet, lather, rinse. Her *and* her ball. It became fluorescent again. She was delighted. I threw it down the beach for her to race after. Airdry.

Snookums hadn't had a bath at the beach yet, but she'd been watching and waiting for her turn. I set the jug beside her in the shallow water, poured some shampoo into my hands, then ran my hands along her little body, scooping up water as needed to work up a lather. She licked the white foaming soap off her leg. Ugh. She shook, and since I hadn't yet rinsed her, sent flecks of soap all over me. Just as well. I smeared them into my tshirt and pants, adding more from the jug.

She hadn't actually swum yet either, preferring to splish splash along the water's edge.

"Chum!" I called our resident lifeguard.

He came swimming toward me with his ball in his mouth. I took his ball and shoved it into my pocket. I left Snookums standing in the shallow water and started walking out, encouraging her to follow me. She wasn't sure. Chum stood beside her, encouraging and reassuring. He took a few steps into the deeper water as well. She still wasn't sure.

I went back to her, picked her up, and carried her in my arms until I was up to my waist. Chum was swimming circles around us, showing her how it was done. I eased her into the water, supporting her as her little legs started pumping. She grinned. I gradually supported her less and less, and eventually she was swimming all on her own. I dropped down and immersed myself. Rinse.

She made a circle back toward me, then, assured that I was still there, swam toward Chum. And, possibly inspired by the pet store parking lot events, onto his back. He continued swimming, Snookums still on his back like a baby loon on mama. Interesting.

Once out into the deeper water, he let himself sag, and Snookums was on her own again. She swam a little bit, then climbed back onto his back. He turned and swam back toward me a bit, then sagged again. Snookums swam back to me on her own. I picked her up. She giggled.

Then I set her into the water again and started walking back to shore, Snookums swimming beside me all the way.

And then I threw Chum's ball for him, again out as far as I could. Such a good dog.

Hunk and Spunky Doo were next. Both had very short coats, so even though they were in the back with Carson, I assumed they weren't suffused through and through with the stink. Which was just as well, since, at least in Spunky Doo's case, I'm not at all convinced I got every part of him.

Finally I turned to Carson again, still lying on the beach. I went to her, picked her up, and the jug, then walked back out. I sat down in the shallow water with her in my lap and proceeded to carefully shampoo her chin, her muzzle, the fur around her eyes, her ears—I even rubbed my shampooed fingers inside her ears. Then I shampooed her under parts. And her tail. And under her tail. And between her toes. On each paw. I was determined to cover every part of her. Her headache must have started receding, because this time she swam around a bit. Rinse.

Bath time over, I started walking along the beach. Airdry set on slow. I threw Kessie's ball along the shore for her, again and again, and I threw Chum's ball into the water for him, again and again. Snookums did her usual splish splash thing along the water line, and Spunky Doo did his usual race ahead, race back, race ahead thing. Hunk wasn't interested in playing in the water today, so he just walked beside me, as did Carson.

When we got to the ice cream place, I realized I didn't have my wallet. I said as much to Shane, the university student who helped run the place every summer.

"No problem, I know you're good for it."

"Great, thanks!"

Mint, Butter Pecan, Peanut Butter Swirl, Tiger Tail Licorice, Espresso Express and—Carson was interested. That was a good sign. A very good sign, since ice cream could be a headache trigger of its own. I asked for a taster of Vanilla. Keep it simple. She agreed. Vanilla it was. And Triple Chocolate Brownie Fudge for myself. Because I can, I told Spunky Doo. Again.

We finished our cones, Snookums finished our faces, taking special care with Carson's, and we headed back.

I had no idea what time it was, so we just sat in the sun until Sam brought the car back. It was, as promised, completely unscented. Still a bit wet, but then so were we.

WE WENT HOME AND had some supper. Carson ate well, finishing up an entire bowl full of kibble, which I took as a very good sign. Kessie showed her how to use the doggy door that led into the fenced yard, and Snookums helped me prepare the guest bed, again contributing a little squeaky mouse from her bowlful in the bedroom. I showed Carson that that was her spot, and not surprisingly, since it had been quite a day for her, she lay down immediately. (Well, not quite immediately. She turned around five times pawing at the towel to bunch it up a bit more.) (Apparently I hadn't done it right.)

NEXT MORNING, A LITTLE nose poked my face, gently. Kessie. She'd nudge, then stare, waiting. If I didn't rouse, she'd nudge again, staring and waiting.

I opened my eyes, saw her, and the joy in her eyes, which was reciprocated, and then I saw Carson sitting beside her. Smiling. Carson was smiling. Yay!

She settled in to our routine quite nicely, which was good,

because her people never did call. It seemed Randy would rather have Sherry in his life than Carson, and apparently Sherry would rather smoke and wear perfume than have Carson in her life. Their loss. Carson was a delightful little dog, happy, alert, and well-mannered.

I retrieved her old collar, took the tag off, and threw the collar away. I washed the tag, just to be sure, then wrote my phone number on a piece of paper and taped it to the back. I then threaded a red bandana through the tag ring and tied it around her neck, making a note to buy her new tags and a proper collar.

It occurred to me that if Carson's sense of smell was better than normal, for a dog—after all, many dogs seem to live with smokers and perfume wearers with no problem—we might be able to do something with it. I'd happened to read about the possibility that dogs might be able to detect cancer. Surely they'd do that by smelling it. Could Carson smell cancer? And could I teach her to let me know when she did? It was an intriguing idea.

I called the local hospital and spoke to the head nurse of the cancer ward. Until that day, I didn't know that our hospital even *had* a cancer ward. She thought my idea had potential. I suspect she was willing to try anything that might reduce the number of people who'd been diagnosed, by traditional means, too late.

We arranged for a room in the basement to be totally disinfected, to become as much as possible scent-free. Then I set up a schedule asking for volunteers—people who'd been diagnosed as having cancer and people who knew they were cancer-free.

Soon after that, we were on our way to the hospital for our first day of training. As we approached the designated room, I heard a loud and angry conversation coming from within. So I paused before entering, to see what the issue was, hoping it wasn't someone already making fun of Carson and my idea.

"I'm just saying that when you say shit like that—'I thank God he spared her, we're so blessed'—what does that say about the rest of us who die from it? We're *not* blessed? God didn't care enough about *us* to spare *us*?"

I took a step forward, but the woman wasn't done.

"And she didn't recover because you prayed for her. She recovered because the cancer stopped spreading. Probably because of the treatment she received. Has your precious little group never prayed for someone who *didn't* survive? How do you explain that?"

I started forward again, but—

"You know what *I'm* tired of?" Another voice. Male this time. "'*Fight it*—you've got to fight the cancer, Don!' Because then when I get worse, or die, it's *my* fault. Like I wasn't fighting hard enough!"

"Yeah." Another woman. "You don't fight cancer. Or any other illness. You endure it. You treat it. You prevent it in the first place. Why isn't the government getting rid of all the carcinogens in our environment? Instead of handing out little pink ribbons."

"Oh don't get me started on those little pink ribbons!" Yet another woman. "Why they think they need to prettify breast cancer is beyond me. Do they think we can't take it otherwise? It's all pink this and pink that, like they're trying to make it all nice. All girly. First, we're not girls. Second, it's not nice. It's life-threatening. It makes you get rid of chunk after chunk of your body. I don't see them putting cute little ribbons on gangrene."

"That's because gangrene isn't sexy. Breasts are sexy. That's what they're capitalizing on. I swear it's just an excuse to get boobs in the media. When's the last time you saw a brown ribbon campaign for colon cancer? Which, by the way, kills more of us than breast cancer."

"Like wearing a ribbon does anything. For anything."

Another silence. Again, I stepped forward to enter—

"Speaking of pink, have you been to a Home Hardware lately?"

Loud guffaws.

"Those pink rakes? And screwdrivers? Like we've been avoiding raking the leaves and making small repairs all these years because the tools were navy blue and black."

"Yeah, men are the color-phobes—no offense—not us. They won't go near a pink screwdriver."

"It's all about maintaining the divide. Men on this side. Women on that side. What the hell for?"

"Either that or it's fucking patronizing. It's not the lack of pink toolbelts that's been keeping us out of the trades."

Another pause in the conversation. I stepped forward and into the room.

"Hi," I said. "I'm Brett, and this is Carson." I thanked them all for coming, then explained what I was trying to do, essentially that I hoped Carson would smell something similar with each one of them, and then not smell that something with the next roomful of people.

I walked her from one person to the next, asking at each one "Cancer?", then putting her right paw on their foot, which would be her way of telling me 'yes' (I'd decided against a bark for obvious reason), then giving her a treat for getting it right.

Half an hour later, the room was full of people who didn't have cancer. "Cancer?" I asked at each one and did *not* put her paw on their foot, then gave her a treat.

Half an hour later, another room full of people with cancer. And then another roomful of people without cancer.

WE DID THIS EVERY day after our afternoon adventure with the crew. I was afraid she might be too tired to concentrate, but she wasn't. I made sure to vary all the variables. I included men and women, people of all ages, people with different kinds of cancer, people with different stages of cancer.

I almost made the mistake of teaching her to identify those who'd had chemotherapy, until I thought to ask about that. In the first couple rooms full of people with cancer, all of them had had chemo, and I suspected that that would change one's smell. So I started being sure to include people who had not had chemo, and switched to her left paw. Just to be sure.

I didn't reprimand her for mistakes, since I wasn't confident they *were* mistakes. Perhaps the cancer had gone, and the person didn't know yet. Or perhaps the person had cancer. And didn't know yet.

Then I started her on mixed groups and didn't find out myself who had cancer and who didn't until after Carson made her decision, just in case I was subconsciously cueing her. We'd go around the room, and at each person, I'd ask Carson, "Cancer?", and we'd wait for her response. Then I asked the person. Again, I rewarded Carson when she was right, but just sort of ignored her when she was wrong. In case she wasn't.

ONE DAY, AN ORDERLY was waiting for us outside the room. He looked like a football player, and I could see how his muscle would be put to good use here.

"Are you the person who's teaching the dog to smell cancer?" he asked.

"Not quite," I replied. "I'm hoping Carson can already smell cancer. As well as a million other things. I'm trying to teach her which one of those million things I want her to tell us about."

"Cool. Is it working?"

Carson stepped up to the man, and put her left paw on his foot.

He looked at me.

"Do you have cancer?"

He nodded. "Hodgkin's Lymphoma. Stage two."

"Then I guess it's working." I would've smiled, but—the man had cancer.

"Wow." He crouched and started petting her. "You are a fantastic little dog, do you know that?" She wagged her tail. Of course she knew that. "She's your dog?" He looked up at me.

"Not really." I told him Carson's story.

"So does that mean you're looking for someone to adopt her?" he asked.

I hadn't really thought about it. Well, I had, but— "Are you interested?"

"Yes. Yes, I am," he crouched again and resumed petting her. "You have a lovely coat," he told her. "Oh, I knew you'd like that," he was stroking her forehead, up from between her eyes.

"I could continue to train her," he looked up at me. "I mean, it's perfect. I work here, in the cancer ward, as an orderly. Tim Muldoon," he reached up to shake my hand. "I'm here every day. So she could come to work with me, every day. I could—how exactly are you teaching her to tell the difference?"

I explained my method. And surreptitiously observed Carson while I did so. She was almost purring.

"I've been keeping notes of everything," I said. "But I don't have enough data yet to determine whether she can smell only certain kinds of cancer. Or only when it gets to a certain stage. I'm also wondering about whether she's smelling chemotherapy or other treatments instead of cancer."

"I haven't had any chemo," he glanced up at me.

"Okay, that's encouraging."

"But there are other treatments that surely leave a stink, so to speak."

"Yeah, I figured."

"You know," he said, standing up, "police train their drug sniffing dogs with a kit. It has a bunch of different scents, each on a strip of paper in a sealed bottle or something. I wonder if we could do the same thing. If different cancers really do have different smells, and there's no reason to assume otherwise... I'll talk to the people here in the lab. I swear Ellen is a wizard, maybe she can come up with an equivalent, a cancer detection kit for Carson to use."

"That would be great!" Why didn't I think of that?

I looked down at Carson, still considering his request.

"Do you smoke?" I should've asked that at the beginning.

Tim laughed. "God, no. And I don't wear Chanel No. 5 either," he said. To Carson. "No perfume, no cologne, I'll even switch to unscented soap and deodorant."

"And you're sure you want a dog in your life?"

"I am," he looked down at Carson, who was actually sitting closer to him now than to me. "I'm sure I want Carson in my life."

"But what about when—"

"My prognosis is very good. And with Carson, it'll be even better."

I was thinking quickly. I knew next to nothing about this person. Then I told myself, once again, take your cue from the dog. And Carson knew—Carson knew he was perfect.

"Okay, but I don't want to just leave her here, now, with you. That feels too much like I'm just abandoning her."

"It does. Why don't—"

"When do you get off?"

"Actually, I just got off. That's why I came down here. To wait for you."

"Oh. Okay. Then how about we drive over to the pet store and the three of us will pick out a bunch of stuff for her. I didn't bring anything from where she was before, and I haven't actually gotten around to even buying her a collar yet. As you can see." I nodded to her red bandana. "Then we can drive to your place, we can get her settled in, and then I'll say my goodbyes."

"That sounds great, doesn't it, Carson?" Tim bent down and they snuggled. "We can get you a new collar, and a leash, and a bowl, *two* bowls," he corrected himself, "one for your food and one for water, and some toys..." he babbled on as best he could between licks. "You didn't have *any* toys at your old house? Well, then, we'll get you *lots and lots* of toys, we'll fill our house with toys, yes we will..."

4

ROSIE

"Hello, are you the dog walker?" The woman sounded stressed, tired, sad, and hopeful.

"Yes, I guess so." I sounded stupid.

"I'm calling from the local shelter, and we've got a dog here we're hoping you'll add to your roster."

Oh. "But don't you have someone who comes every day to take all your dogs for a walk?" I thought the local high school provided a co-op student every term to do just that. And, well, to clean out the kennels and provide general help while learning enough to figure out if they wanted to become a vet or a vet assistant. Used to be we'd just volunteer.

"We do, yes, but Rosie's very depressed and refuses to—she won't even get up anymore. We're hoping a new person, a new bunch of dogs—"

"I'll be there in an hour," I interrupted. She had me at 'she won't even get up anymore'.

So I called everyone. I had a lot of faith in Snookums, but I called Chum, Spunky Doo, Hunk, and even Little Miss—hopefully one of them would somehow, or all of them together would—or, yes, I said to Kess, maybe the sight of a *brand new* fluorescent green tennis ball would do it! I went to the closet and let her get a new one out of the somewhat depleted 100-ball pack.

CHUM, SPUNKY DOO, HUNK—as soon as we turned right, not left, at the critical intersection, he broke into a howl. (Her person had relented. Finally.) Little Miss was sitting on the front yard primly, though barely so. She contained herself until we actually pulled into her driveway, then let loose and got up, wiggling her behind just a bit.

Hunk leapt out when I opened the back door, ran toward her, but stopped a few feet short. Something was different. She smelled —different. He approached and started sniffing. No... no... no... no...yes! His nose was in her underparts. This is different! Something is different here, something happened here!!

"Could you please not let him do that?" Little Miss' person had appeared at the front door.

I gently pulled Hunk's nose out of Little Miss' crotch. "Later," I said to him.

ONCE I PULLED INTO the small parking lot, I put Snookums' snuggly thing on, put her in it, then went to the shelter's front door, leaving the rest of them in the car, all windows open, with strict instructions not to jump out—there was no stink to escape this time, but I felt I needed to point that out to Spunky Doo.

Merrill led me to the back, to Rosie's cage. A mottled beige greyhound was curled up in the corner. She looked like a despondent lump of meat. As I went inside her pen, I saw the fresh scars along the length of her back.

"What happened?" I asked, quietly.

"We don't know for sure," Merrill said, just as quietly. "Someone found her at the racetrack, lying beside the trash can. Looked like she'd been whipped half to death, then kicked. Repeatedly. We had to suture—her back was in shreds. And she had several broken ribs."

"My god. Who would do such a thing?"

"An owner who had a lot of money on a race? Angry because she placed second instead of first?"

So he whipped her? Because she didn't run fast enough?

I thought of the scene in *The Piano* where the guy chops off the woman's finger. With a single stroke, he destroyed a life. He'd taken not just a finger, but her source of—not just pleasure, not even just bliss, but passion. Playing the piano was—it was what she lived for.

At least, I thought, Rosie's owner hadn't broken her legs.

Rosie looked at me then, and for a moment, I saw her eyes flicker. I saw the hurt in her eyes. The betrayal. She'd run as fast as she could. Those beautiful brown eyes, so full of hurt and betrayal. Then they went dull again. Flat.

"Will she ever run again, do you think?" I asked.

"Doubtful. My guess is she'll fall apart if she gets anywhere near a track."

"So you've had her for how long?"

"Months. The wounds had to heal, and we wanted her immobile anyway for her ribs to heal. Then when she was ready, she started to join the others for the daily walk around the block, but I guess it was just too depressing, given what she used to do. Karen, our walker, tried to take her by herself a couple times, breaking into a jog, but it was a no go. Rosie refused to do more than walk. Then she started refusing to do even that. She hasn't left her cage at all for the past week. We started to think euthanasia may be the kindest thing we could do, but then someone heard of you, and now that her back and ribs are completely healed, we thought maybe you and your pack could get her walking again..."

"Actually, I think I can do better than that." I had an idea.

But for now, I set Snookums down at my feet. She tiptoed to the corner to where Rosie lay. She knew. Snookums knew something was very wrong here, something was very sad here. She gently crawled over Rosie's folded up hind legs, no doubt thinking there must be more than two of them, and tucked herself into the space she'd made. After a while, Rosie lifted her head to look at Snookums. Snookums smiled and gave her a lick, right on the tip of her long pointed nose. She thumped her little tail hopefully. Then she crawled out of Rosie's hind legs and clambered over her fore legs. Rosie kept moving her legs to accommodate Snookums, then finally decided that what with all that movement, she may as well just get up.

So Rosie slowly unfolded herself, and stood. Snookums looked up. Way up. And giggled.

WITH SNOOKUMS BACK IN her snuggly, and Rosie on a leash, we walked out to the car. Oh. Right. I hadn't anticipated adding a greyhound to the pack.

I really should've sold the car. And gotten a bus. Or something.

I set Snookums into the driver's seat beside Kessie, then walked around the car, considering all possible rearrangements. There was no way around it.

"You'll have to get in the trunk," I told Spunky Doo.

He was delighted. So was Hunk.

"No, just kidding," I said. "Your brain can't afford *any* oxygen deprivation."

I stuffed him into the passenger seat foot space. He had, after all, fit into the firefighers' bucket. More or less. Chum and Snookums would just have to be careful not to step onto him. Or not.

Rosie got in beside Little Miss and Hunk, who were already sitting as close together as possible. So it worked.

Even so, since I happened to see a car dealership two blocks later, I pulled in. A salesperson came out immediately.

"Hi," I gestured at my little car full of dogs. "I'm in the market for something roomier. What are they making these days?"

She looked at Hunk, Little Miss, Rosie, Snookums, Kessie, and Chum. And Spunky Doo, who somehow managed to pop his head up.

"Well, you could go with an extra-long SUV. Or a minivan. Do you want a back seat or would you rather have all open space behind the front?" Open space would mean a lot of inadvertent jostling. Or it might mean, on longer trips, that they could stretch out and lay down.

"Can I have both? A back seat that could fold down?"

"Yes. We can get that."

"Do different makes have different sizes of seat? I mean, see where their front paws are? When they're sitting?" I pointed to Hunk and Little Miss. "Their paws are so close to their body, they're more teetery than they want to be. Another couple inches of seat would make the bigger ones more comfortable. More stable."

"Hm. No one's ever asked about that before. But I do know that some makes suit taller people better, so...I'll look into that," she started making notes. "Failing that, we may be able to get some sort of custom-fitting boxes that can be put in the footwells. You never transport people?"

Silly question. I ignored it.

"And the front seat," I said a few seconds later, "can I get, you know, how they used to be all one? Without the gear shift in the middle?"

"A bench seat. I can look into that," she made a note. "Air conditioning, of course?"

"Yes. And lots of windows. That open. Remote-controlled. Individually."

"You'll want the back window to open as well?"

"That'd be good."

"What about a sunroof?"

I thought of Spunky Doo, and his purple octopus head. "Sure," I said, "that could be fun."

TWENTY MINUTES LATER, WE were at the beach. Free at least, free at last, thank god—Spunky Doo took off as soon as he wriggled his way out. He could've waited until Chum had gotten out, but it was more fun not to. Chum and Kessie followed him, after a short, but frantic, search for Kessie's tennis ball and Chum's beach ball, both of which had gotten dislodged from where they'd been set, carefully on the seat.

I opened the back door next for Hunk and Little Miss, who got out on the same side, of course, and waited, glued together, until I walked around to open Rosie's door. She got out and came with us, reluctantly, even with Snookums' encouragement, as we walked down the short path to long expanse of sandy beach.

We were in luck. There she was, running, far in the distance. The sprinter I often saw. Charmaine.

Rosie—unbelievably, given typical canine eyesight—also saw her. I swear I felt the longing in every cell of her body.

"Go," I whispered, and gave her the slightest of nudges.

She did. And Oh. My. God. It was— She ran on joy. Her fuel was pure joy. She didn't run so much as soar across the beach in a series of split leaps. Her body was wonderfully aerodynamic, from her pointed nose, to her slightly broader muzzle, to her slightly broader yet skull, to her narrow but powerful shoulders. And her stride was as wonderfully efficient. Every hurdler struggling with the least bit of vertical movement would just pack it in if they saw her.

Then my jaw dropped. Rosie had caught up with Charmaine. I watched as she overtook her. Charmaine upped her speed. Ten meters from the marker she'd set, Rosie upped her speed as well. And won. Rosie won!

As soon as she was able to straighten up—having doubled over as soon as she came to a stop—Charmaine looked around for Rosie's owner. I waved. She returned the wave.

Rosie started loping back toward us then, Charmaine jogging behind. When Rosie got back to me, I praised her to the hilt. We all did. Yes, we all saw you RUN! And you WON! Rosie turned then and saw Charmaine still in motion. I raised my hand, made a circle, pointed back down the beach, then made pathetic running motions with my arms. Charmaine understood. She turned and broke into another sprint.

"Go," I whispered again to Rosie. She took off again, running full out. This time, when she caught up to Charmaine, she did not overtake her. She just matched Charmaine's speed. She didn't need to win again. She just needed to run. Beside someone. Preferably, with someone.

And Charmaine was the perfect someone. I'd met her here a while ago and discovered that she was a student at the local university and a sprinter on their track team. Every second day she was here, putting herself through a grueling routine of ten 100-meter sprints, then ten 200-meter sprints. In the sand. It sounds idyllic, going for a run on the beach, but it's frickin' hard. I tried it. Once. Sand is great because it cushions your impact, but it gives you nothing to push off of. That's why no one wants to be her training partner.

But the benefits are immense. Charmaine said that after running on the beach, running on a track feels like you have springs on your feet. Without any extra effort, her stride increases almost 25%. And, so, her times decrease by almost the same percentage.

Charmaine was determined to make the national team. It looked very possible, given her times this season, and her age. Not to mention her dedication. And the glow she had going when she was out here. She loved running fast, that's all there was to it. She was born to race. And would do so whether she made the team or not.

"Hey," she said when she reached us. I noted that Rosie had stayed with her this time, walking beside her as she jogged. (Yes, *walking* beside her as she *jogged*.)

"Hey," I said back, throwing Kessie's ball back up the beach, then Chum's ball back into the water.

"She's magnificent," Charmaine murmured as she ran her hands along Rosie's shoulders to her flanks, caressing, massaging the solid muscle under the silky coat. Rosie's eyes met mine. They were glistening. And oh god, I wept.

"Isn't she?"

Rosie wasn't much to look at, her coat actually looked like it had stains on it, but neither of us was talking about that.

"She's a new addition to your crew?" Charmaine asked, nodding to Hunk and Little Miss, and bending down to say hi to Snookums.

"Not exactly, she's from the shelter."

"You mean— I could adopt her? She could be mine?"

"And you could be hers," I said. I told her Rosie's story then, what little I knew of it.

"Do you know the guy's name?" Charmaine asked in a tight

voice, "Or where he lives?" Her hand reached down protectively to Rosie. "I have friends who would love to kick the shit out of him. I'd even buy a whip for the occasion."

"If I knew," I said, "I'd tell you." And I realized that I meant it.

"She's perfect," Charmaine said then, turning her attention back to Rosie. "She didn't trip me like almost every other dog I've ever run with."

Speaking of which, I looked around for Spunky Doo. Ah, there he was. Tripping himself. And laughing about it.

"And she just—*just*—kept ahead of me, pulling me forward a little faster. I increased my speed, she increased hers. But just enough so I still felt it was possible to overtake her."

"You'd never overtake her." Pigs would never fly.

"Nor would I want to. After what she's been through? She's felt enough defeat to last her lifetime."

Oh wow, please adopt her.

"How old is she, do you think?"

"I don't know. Two? Three?"

"I live in a townhouse," Charmaine was thinking out loud. "There's a bunch of us from the team."

I nodded.

"But I'm away a lot. At meets."

"Is everyone who lives with you on the team?"

"Well, no. Celine isn't. I could ask her if she'd look after Rosie when I'm not there."

I nodded again.

"I couldn't take her with me, right? She'd freak at the sight of a track?"

"That'd be my guess. What about an indoor track though?" I wondered. "Do you think she'd enjoy racing on an indoor track?"

"I dunno. They're banked. Wouldn't that wreck her legs?"

"Probably. Yeah. And maybe we shouldn't risk it in any case," I said. "It's enough that she ran today. That she will run on the beach. With you. That's amazing enough."

"It is. You are," she said to Rosie, giving her another full body stroke. Rosie leaned into her.

"Okay," Charmaine looked up at me, beaming. It was settled. "So, you'll take her back to the shelter and—"

"Do you want to keep her now?" I asked. "It might—"

"Yes."

I grinned. I gave her the name and address of the shelter, so she could go do the paperwork.

"I don't actually know if you have to pay an adoption fee or something," I said. "If you do, and it's too much—starving student and all—call me, and I'll take care of it." I gave her one of my cards.

"Okay, thanks."

I bent down to say good-bye to Rosie. She rested her long muzzle against my cheek. Thank you.

"And if Celine says no, do *not* take her to a kennel. And do *not* miss your meet. Call me. I'll look after her."

"Seriously?"

"Seriously."

"Thank you."

"Thank you!"

Charmaine turned then, since she still had several sprints to do. Rosie turned with her. And never looked back.

5

BISCUIT

My new car had arrived! Woohoo! I had just gotten a call from Heather, at the car dealership. So I told her I'd be in to pick it up that afternoon, on our way to the dog park. I thought I'd take the whole crew for a test drive. It was for them, after all.

AS SOON AS I pulled in to the lot, I saw it. Cars are never quite as shiny as they are when they're new. Especially if they're metallic red. I parked my shabby, decidedly unshiny, car beside it, then looked at Snookums.

"Are you sure you've outgrown your carsickness?"

She looked worried.

I immediately felt bad. She was such a sensitive soul; my tone had been too stern.

"Oh sweetheart, it's okay if you haven't," I snuggled her apologetically.

She squiggled. All was well with the world again.

"Stay," I said to everyone, unnecessarily, except for Spunky Doo, and got out.

I heard Spunky Doo's nose hit the glass. Ouch.

Heather had seen me pull in and was already at the new vehicle.

"So what do you think?" she asked, smiling.

"I think I want to take it home," I smiled back.

She opened the front door. "Bench seat."

She opened a back door. "Custom-made footwell boxes," she said, reaching in and pulling one out, "that double as steps." She set it on the ground by the open door.

"Perfect!" I said with delight, seeing that the step up was greater than with my car.

She went around to the back and opened the hatch door. Roomy. She went back around to the other side, opened the back door, and put down a seat. Roomier.

"And the back hatch window opens?" I asked.

"It does." She demonstrated. "As do all of the others, of course, all remote-controlled, individually, as you wanted."

"Perfect."

"And," she said, her eyes twinkling, "I had the upholstery stain-treated, but I also," she opened one of the footwell boxes, which, I hadn't realized until then, doubled as storage space—for leashes, water bottles, portable water dishes...paper towels, wet-wipes—cool!—"had durable, washable, seat covers made for you!" She shook out a long piece of fabric, elasticized all around, reinforced at the corners. "Ta-dah!" It was covered in pawprints of all sizes.

"So perfect!"

I followed Heather into her office to complete the paperwork, then returned to move all of my stuff, and all of the dogs, from my old car to my new—dogmobile!

Spunky Doo, ever up for a challenge, cleared the step box in one sloppy leap and smashed into the far door. Ouch.

Little Miss primly stepped onto the box and into the car. Hunk followed. I noticed right away that Little Miss had her front paws on the smaller box that fit over the hump. (Spunky Doo's paws were on the side window and the back ledge.) Hunk had also noticed and watched carefully as I picked up the step box and fitted it into the footwell. He immediately moved his front paws forward onto it. And gave a sigh of satisfaction. I swear he did.

Chum didn't need the step box, but Kessie neatly leapfrogged from the pavement to the box to the seat. Walked right over to the driver's side.

Snookums got airlifted in her snuggly onto the space between them. Ever the baby.

I went around to the driver's side, got in after them, adjusted the windows, adjusted the mirrors, and looked with satisfaction at the extra room in the back.

I was ready for a great dane.

BISCUIT WAS A CHIHUAHUA.

He was standing on the middle cushion of a green couch, tail wagging, when I entered the room. He had a cute little face. A cute little happy face. His person, Jan, seventy-something and living in a seniors' apartment complex, had called me because he'd gradually lost interest in going for a walk, then a couple days ago, refused altogether. He wasn't even running around the small apartment like usual. Which would explain why he looked more like a bun than a biscuit. A cream-white yummy bun.

But he didn't look lame. In fact, he looked pretty sturdy standing there, wagging his teeny tiny little tail. He didn't seem to be favoring any of his legs, and there was no noticeable swelling or other indication of injury.

Given said wagging tail, he didn't look sick either. His cute little happy face was not in pain.

"Has anything changed about your route?" I asked Jan. "Maybe a new dog has moved in and Biscuit's afraid to walk by?"

"No, we always go the same way" she said. Then muttered, "That way, I don't get lost."

I looked at her.

"Want some advice about getting old?" she asked. "Don't."

Ah.

"Want a margarita?" she asked next. "I was just about to make a batch."

What, no cup of tea? I looked in vain for doilies, a half-knitted sweater, and a profusion of knick knacks. What I saw was a wall full of books. Cool.

"I'd love a margarita."

I sat on one of the two blue chairs facing the couch, on which Biscuit still stood, still wagging his tail at me. He had not yet come to check me out. Interesting.

There were two hexagonal tables set between the couch and chairs, instead of the usual long living room table. Odd, I thought. But then who am I to comment on anyone's interior design. I didn't even have a living room.

I picked up one of the several books sitting on one of the tables. Catherine MacKinnon. *Feminism Unmodified.*

"I don't know if it's as good as her others," Jan said, handing me the promised margarita, her hand shaking a little—early

Parkinson's?—then sitting in the other chair. I noticed that Biscuit didn't jump into her lap. "My eyes seem to have given up altogether on print."

"Have you tried a magnifier?" I'd seen a neat whole-page magnifying plate thing advertised on tv that, frankly, I expected having to use myself one day. I took a sip of the lovely frosted green drink.

"Yes, but—"

I waited.

"I also don't give a damn anymore."

"Anymore?"

"Do the math," she replied. "I'm seventy-five now. So I was in my twenties during the sixties. I was on the forefront of peace and free love," she grimaced, "a bunch of us actually went to the States for the civil rights marches, I was one of Morgentaler's defenders in the 70s back here in Canada, I came of age with Morgan, Millett, Firestone, Solanas, Dworkin, Greer, Steinem..."

What was that like? I wanted to know, thirstily. Did you actually meet any of those women? And so what do you think of the American law forcing women to look at an ultrasound of the embryo before they abort...

"And now?" I asked.

"It's like it never happened. Personally. And politically."

I nodded. "I take it you're not a fan of *Desperate Housewives*."

She snorted.

"Yesterday, I clicked on the new stations channel," she nodded to the tv in the corner of the room. "There are five. Three are porn. Men being serviced by women, men being entertained by being serviced by women..."

I'd seen that. The other two were kids' channels.

"So," I tried to change the channel, "is he eating as usual?" I nodded to Biscuit—Bun—and realized it was a stupid question.

"Yes, no change there," she took a sip of her margarita.

"And the day he stopped—anything unusual happen that day or the day before? He didn't fall or anything?"

"Not that I saw."

She set her drink down, then got up and picked him up—and I saw the problem.

"His nails!" I cried out, aghast. They were so long, they were starting to curl. "When was the last time you cut his nails?"

"I—" She looked at his feet. Then looked at me. Then looked at his feet again, before setting him carefully back onto the soft cushion of the couch.

"I can't believe I didn't notice," she finally said, sitting back down. "I've never had a dog before. Or a cat. Or anything. I was always away somewhere...you never knew when you might find yourself in jail overnight..."

"But—"

"Biscuit is Carol's dog. She died. A few months ago."

Ah. That would explain a few things. "And Carol is..."

"She lived down the hall. I looked after Biscuit a couple times when she went in for surgery, and, well, last time, she didn't come back. She loved Biscuit like you wouldn't believe. What was I supposed to do, drop him off at the humane society? Look at him!" She grinned sheepishly. "He grows on you, the cute little bugger."

Indeed. He gazed at us with his cute little button eyes—

"But he seems so happy," I couldn't help saying.

"Now, yes..." She seemed to be realizing this for the first time. She smiled slightly. "But at first—maybe it was more than a few months ago," she revised, considering. "We still have to walk by Carol's door on our way out, so he can check, make sure she hasn't come back. Poor thing."

"Not so poor," I said. "He has you."

"Yeah." Another grudging smile.

He has you wrapped around his cute little paw, I thought.

"So when was the last time you took him to the vet?" I asked, coming back to the problem.

"I did do that," she said, "because he wasn't eating at first. So he's all up to date with his shots, and I think the vet must have cut his nails, but—"

"His nails need to be cut more often than once a year."

"Yes, I see that now." She was still angry with herself.

"So…do you just want to take him to the vet? To get his nails clipped?"

"Well…"

I didn't understand why she was hesitant.

"They charge so much…"

Ah.

"See that's the problem with not having had a 'real' job," she said bitterly. "I was always part-time here, temp there— It doesn't make for a good pension plan."

I understood. And saw my future flash before my eyes.

And realized that it had been a while since the temp agency had called me…

"I'm lucky to be here, such as it is," she glanced around the small apartment. "The rent's reasonable, and everything's included, but…"

"It's not where you expected to be at this point."

"No, it's not." She took a good slug of her margarita.

I thought about calling the vet and shaming him into charging just five bucks to cut his nails once a month. But maybe even getting to and from the vet was a problem. Did she have a car? A valid licence, given her eyesight? What had she done, smuggled him onto the bus? Could she handle the step up, I wondered, without a cool step box? Had she taken a taxi? An expensive taxi?

I got up and sat beside Biscuit on the couch, then reached out to take a closer look—and he bit me.

Well, since I didn't pull away, he didn't actually break skin. But he changed my mind about suggesting that she just cut his nails herself. At least this first time.

"Tell you what. I have a spare pair of nail clippers," I assumed Biscuit hadn't come with nail clippers. Or, if he had, that he'd since eaten them. His teeth were still bared at me. "I'll go home and get them, we'll cut his nails today, and then maybe he'll let you do it from now on."

She looked doubtful, even a little fearful. She who had fought for women's right to abortion.

Note to self. Don't grow old.

SO I DROVE TO the nearest pet shop and headed for their grooming aisle. Would she be more comfortable with the guillotine style of clippers or the scissors style? Biscuit's nails were small, so the scissors would work. But the guillotine was quicker. I could see him pulling away as soon as—I could see him pulling away. I took one of each.

And, because I could see him pulling away, I also took some Kwik Stop powder.

Then I went to the treat aisle and picked out three different kinds. Mandatory.

Then I spent fifteen minutes looking for a pair of thick canvas gloves. In vain.

"Where do you keep your gloves?" I asked at the checkout.

"I don't think we carry gloves," she replied with a clear lack of interest. She was busy doing her nails. Ironically.

"Dogs bite. When they're upset," I added. "And you don't carry gloves?"

"Don't think so," she replied, filing away.

"Could you find out? For sure?" This wasn't the store I usually went to. And it wasn't about to become the store I usually went to.

"I can't leave the register."

Oh for pete's sake. If I knew the hardware store I'd passed also carried nail clippers, Kwik Stop, and treats, I would have left without making any of my purchases.

Five minutes later, I was looking at twenty different kinds of gloves. I considered getting the heavy rubber ones that went up to my elbow—what the hell were they for?—but decided they'd make me too clumsy. I had noticed that all of Biscuit's nails were white, which would make it easy to see the quick, but if I cut too close, he would never let anyone cut his nails again. Ever. Plus, Jan would be spot-cleaning blood from her furniture and carpets for days. I bought a pair of lightweight canvas ones.

I considered going home to get Kessie and Snookums as teaching aids. But then decided their presence might just make Biscuit more excited. Nails are best clipped when dogs are decidedly unexcited. Tired. Asleep even.

BACK IN JAN'S APARTMENT, I sat on the couch beside Biscuit, put my gloves on, and opened one of the bags of treats. Tried to open one of the bags of treats. I pulled off my gloves and tried again. Succeeded. He came to investigate. I baby-talked him and gave him a treat. So far, so good. I put the gloves back on.

Then I picked him up. Tried to pick him up. He leapt away. But seemed to regret it. Poor thing, I was surprised half of his toes weren't sprained.

I cornered him, literally, on the couch, and took hold of one of his paws with my left hand, guillotine clippers ready in my right. It was then that I realized the scissors would be better, since his nails had begun curling.

I cornered him, again, took hold of one of his paws with my left hand, again, scissors clippers ready in my right.

He resisted. I insisted. It was for his own good. He squirmed and pulled and I knew there was no way.

I put the clippers down, picked him up, and flipped him onto his back—glad he wasn't a Great Dane—forcing him into the classic submission position. Often this worked: dogs knew submission when they felt it.

Biscuit wasn't feeling it. He squirmed and struggled and again, I knew there was no way. No doubt he thought I was going to cut his feet off.

I reconsidered. I baby-talked a bit more, and offered another treat. He wasn't falling for that this time. He growled at me. I smiled. I couldn't help it. It was such a cute little growl. I know, I know, it really sucks to be not taken seriously…but it *was* a cute little growl.

I stood up, reconsidered the situation, then picked him up and tucked him under my left arm like a football. A cream-white yummy little football.

I reached around with my left hand and grabbed his left front paw. He pulled it back. I let him. He discovered he could pull back only so far. And it didn't occur to him to push out. Aha. I had him.

He reached down and tried to bite me again. To no avail. I gave him another thirty seconds. When it seemed he couldn't come up with any other resistance strategies, I carefully, but quickly, snipped all the toenails on that one paw.

He sprang out of my grip onto the floor. Oh. He took a step forward. Wow. He took another step forward. Then actually picked up his front left paw and looked at it. He looked back at me.

"Do you want me to cut the rest of your nails?" I asked him, holding up the clippers.

He took a step toward me, then held up his right front paw. Wow indeed.

I picked him up and lay him on the couch.

"Stay." I took off my gloves and rubbed his cute little belly.

"Stay," I repeated as I knelt beside him at a right angle. I reached out for his right front paw, and let him pull it back. He couldn't help it. I understood. But then he stayed still. I shifted slightly. Perfect. Excellent view, excellent angle for the clippers.

I explained to Jan, who had been helplessly watching the proceedings, about pressing the paw a little so the nail protruded, not cutting too close to the quick, and trying to make the middle two toe nails the same length. I also explained that his nails should really be shorter, but since the quick had become extended this was all we could do now. If we kept at it, eventually the quick would shrink back, and we could get his nails to where they should be. I also pointed out his dewclaws, which also needed to be clipped. I know she was listening, but...

"Done!" I said, triumphantly, and leaned back.

Biscuit leapt off the couch. He paused for just a moment, just feeling, almost flexing...then broke into a run around the apartment. He did a figure-eight around the two hexagonal tables in the middle of the living room. (So that's what that was all about.) And another. And another. Then he ran into the kitchen and slalomed in and out of the four chairs set at the table. He came back into the living room and jumped onto the couch. Jumped off the couch. Jumped onto the couch. He leapt clear across one of the hexagonal tables onto the chair I'd been in. Then he jumped down onto the floor again and ran around the apartment again.

I got tired just watching him, so I sat back down in the chair. And finished my margarita.

He stopped for a moment in front of me, to catch his breath, panting, his teeny little pink tongue just visible. Then he threw himself down into the play position, and swung his cute little rump to the left and then to the right. Then he jumped up and did a one-eighty, and then another one. The Chihuahua version of the Macarena? It was far better than Bud's version, I had to say.

"So, here you go," I said to Jan, handing the clippers to her.

She took them in her shaking hand, but looked—terrified.

"Tell you what," I said. "I'll come every week or so to cut his nails."

Next time I'd even bring some frosted green nail polish. For Biscuit.

"But I don't—"

I held up my still-steady hand. "In return, I expect margaritas and meaningful conversation." Because God knows there were few enough of those around. Meaningful conversations, not margaritas. Although those were few and far between in my life as well.

We both turned then, hearing the rattle of wind chimes. I had noticed them hung at the door when I came in, surprised that he didn't just bark when he wanted out. Jan smiled. Full out. Definitely wrapped around his cute little paws.

And then, in case we didn't get the message, he pranced—*pranced,* like a miniature Lipizzaner stallion—into the center of the room with his leash in his mouth.

6

WINNER

Several weeks later, we met an australian shepherd at the dog park. Well, we also met its person, Kath, but of the two of them, Winner was clearly the more noteworthy. A young, enthusiastic blue-and-grey australian shepherd, he was quite literally 'born to herd': he was herding my feet as we spoke.

Kath told me, as we walked along the path, me with some difficulty, given the forementioned herding that was going on, that she liked that Winn would herd her kids toward shore when they went swimming at the beach. But he also herded them when they were just playing in the yard. And doing their chores. And watching tv. When she discovered him herding leaves on a windy day, she figured she had to do something.

So she made some calls and discovered that there was a sheep farm nearby that allowed city herding dogs, like Winner, to come out for day visits, to do the real thing.

Sort of. Although australian shepherds are born to herd, they have to be taught to respond to the farmer's directions. Otherwise, they don't know where to herd the sheep *to.* So what Winn was allowed to do was, essentially, just chase sheep.

He loved it.

I'm not so sure about the sheep.

In any case, she started taking him to the farm once a week for an hour of sheer bliss. And that's how she found out there was a Sheep Herding Trial, a competition among real sheep herding dogs, the following weekend. She couldn't go, since she had to work that weekend, but suggested I go. And would I take Winn? He'd love it!

I DIDN'T TELL LITTLE Miss' person we were going to a sheep herding trial. She would've said no. An open field? With barnyard animals trotting about? Absolutely not. Especially since, I saw now, Little Miss had just been to the groomer. Why do people do that to their poodles? Though I had to say, Little Miss didn't seem to mind. She walked to the car—Little Miss, not her person—like she was too sexy for Milan.

I glanced at Hunk. Hard to tell. I'd never seen that expression on a dog before.

Nor did I tell Spunky Doo's people. They'd given a blanket 'yes' to everything, and I assumed that included barnyard animals. Trotting about.

Jocko would have frozen in fear at the open field, Rosie was running on the beach that weekend with Charmaine, Carson was busy being the cure for cancer, and I was afraid Biscuit would get trampled.

Oh well, just the seven of us then.

In my new vehicle, Kess continued to claim my lap, and the air vent, Snookums and Chum continued to have the front seat, but I'd taken to putting Spunky Doo in the back compartment, leaving the back seat for just Hunk and Little Miss. They appreciated it.

When I showed up at Kath's house, Winn was ready, but Kath couldn't find his leash. Just as I was about to say I had an extra in the car, in one of the dandy handy step/storage/ pawrest boxes, she appeared with a short length of bright yellow nylon rope; it had a clip on one end, but was just cut off at the other. I clipped the one end onto Winn's collar, then tied a few knots in the other end, partly to keep it from fraying and partly to give me something to hold onto. And then I put him in the back with Spunky Doo.

As I drove away, up the street, I glanced in my rear view mirror. Winn was herding Spunky Doo into the corner. Then into the other corner. Then back into the first corner. Then into the other other corner. Spunky Doo had no idea what the game was, but he was enjoying it immensely. Judging by the loopy grin on his face. Which was in marked contrast with the intensity on Winn's face.

ALMOST AN HOUR LATER, I pulled off a back road onto a laneway clearly marked—"Sheep Herding Trial". I parked in the spot clearly marked "Parking". So far, so good.

We all got out, piddled—yes, me too, though I used the conveniently present PortaPotty—who the hell approved that name, by the way? Who, over six, calls a washroom, or even a toilet, a 'potty'? No one, that's who. Which confirms my belief that most of the people in marketing, who are mostly men, are infantile. It explains a lot.

Especially since marketing *manufactures* most people's interests, desires, values… We are so doomed.

But in the meantime, we all got out, piddled, then walked toward, then behind, the bleachers set up along the length of a field, passing as we did so a great many makeshift tents set up behind the bleachers. Beside several of these, there was a shepherd straining at its rope anchored to a peg or pacing inside its cage, trying to see the competition, eagerly waiting its turn.

Snookums had to say hello to each of them.

When we finally got to an empty section, I herded the dogs—see, I was getting into the swing of things—up onto the second bench. I had Winner on his rope leash, and he opted for the best seat in the house, on the first bench, more or less between my knees. Everyone else was with me on the second bench. Hunk and Little Miss on my left, Snookums in her snuggly on my lap, Kessie tucked beside me on my right, Chum beside her, and Spunky Doo— Shit. Where was Spunky Doo?

The bench under us heaved.

Of course.

I watched, incredulously, as Spunky Doo climbed onto the bench from underneath it, squiggling between the seat part and the foot part. It took three tries. Neither Hunk nor Little Miss was impressed. I was though. It was a tight fit. And the bench was high enough, he couldn't just push off from the ground. He had to sort of hang on with his front paws and belly up to—

Made it! He grinned at me. I grinned back.

And then we all settled to watch the action on the field.

A man had walked onto the field with an also blue-and-grey shepherd. He carefully took his place—I skimmed the back of the event schedule I'd picked up at the entrance and discovered that the 'handler' (not the 'shepherd'?) had to stay inside a small marked circle—then someone else walked to a pen and opened the gate.

A herd of sheep ran toward us and Little Miss gasped. Gasped? Ah. She was probably thinking the sheep needed a haircut.

Something stylish. Fluff out the ears a bit, shave the back, but leave a little poof on the tail and around the ankles...

The handler said something—we were too far away to hear what—and the dog started racing around in a large circle, making the sheep move back toward the gated pen. Suddenly the dog flattened. The handler had given the 'lie down' command—I was reading the back of the schedule again—either by voice or whistle. Then the dog got up and raced around in the other direction. It was actually very impressive, the way they managed to keep all the sheep together and going just where they wanted them to go. The dog raced turned and raced around in the other direction. Left was 'come by' and right was 'away'. Okay, that would explain why it was harder for them to herd sheep away from the handler than toward the handler. Wouldn't left become right then?

While I tried to figure it out—clearly I wouldn't make a good sheep herding dog—I noticed that Kessie was perplexed as well. She was probably wondering where the tennis ball was. A big field like that, there had to be a tennis ball out there somewhere. She cast her eyes left and right, trying to see where it was.

In the meantime, another dog had taken the field. I think. They were all blue-and-grey shepherds, and I couldn't tell them apart. Does that make me racist?

The second dog raced off in a large circle around the clump of sheep—a far larger circle than necessary I thought, but then what the hell did I know? I did think it plausible that the dog just enjoyed racing around, but it did eventually get the sheep herded into the gated pen.

I wondered what the sheep thought of all of this. You get us into the pen, then you let us out, then you get us back into the pen, then you let us out.

It occurred to me that the last dog would have an advantage, as the sheep by then would surely know what was expected. Actually, wouldn't they know at the beginning what was expected? Hadn't they spent their entire lives being herded into a gated pen? How stupid were they, I wondered.

While I watched the next dog, I realized that the object was not just to herd the sheep into the pen; the dogs were also supposed to herd them around various partial fences and through various closely situated bunches of rocks and tree stumps. Basically, they had to herd them through an obstacle course. Okay, that made it even more impressive. (Herding them *over* partial fences would have been more impressive still.)

The current dog looked like it was having trouble keeping the sheep together, running back and forth behind them, trying to make sure not one escaped the herd. Which is exactly what happened. Then it got its right and left mixed up. You could see the hesitation—it actually started in one direction, then stopped, and pointedly looked at its handler as if confessing its uncertainty and asking for confirmation. Things really began to fall apart then, as the herd split into three different bunches. But they fixed it. The dog and its handler corrected this sorry state of affairs, and received some well-deserved applause. They wouldn't win, since it took so long, but I thought they should be given extra marks for making something so wrong turn out right.

I was struck then by the low-key good nature of the handlers. They were, apparently, saying 'Walk on' and 'That'll do' instead of screaming 'GO!!' and 'STAY!!' which, I thought, would be the case if Americans had invented sheep herding. No one here was going whip a dog if it didn't win.

Giggles rose from the crowd and I noticed then that another dog had taken the field. It was doing the flatten-and-freeze then crawl-forward-and-stalk thing. It was being sneaky. Suddenly one of the sheep—a big one with horns—turned to face it. I was too far away to see 'the eye' but knew what was happening. I'd finished reading the back of the schedule. And I'd seen Winn do the same thing. The dog was staring the sheep down. And no one makes eye contact like an australian shepherd. The dog *demands* connection. I think one of the saddest things in the world would be an australian shepherd going blind. Seeing that blank look in its eyes rather than the intelligence beaming at you like a laser would be absolutely devastating.

It was a pity that herding was being done now by people on dirt bikes and atvs—

Suddenly Kess got it. The sheep was the tennis ball! She tore off the bench onto the field and in seconds, a murmur rose from the crowd. I had stood up to call her back, but then sat right back down. The dog working the sheep had turned to her and was staring *her* down. Okay. Just not *her* tennis ball.

She returned to me, but her stunt gave Spunky Doo an idea. Specifically, the idea of running onto the field. Once there, he started imitating the herding dog. When it tore around the sheep to the right, he tore after it. When it suddenly went flat, he suddenly went flat. Laughter rose from the crowd. When the herding dog sprang up and tore around to the left, Spunky Doo sprang up and tore after it to the left. The dog turned to face Spunky Doo. Spunky Doo turned to face no one. The laughter increased. When the dog suddenly flattened again and started crawling forward, stalking, Spunky Doo flattened and started crawling forward, stalking, his ass end wiggling considerably more than that of the australian shepherd. The crowd cracked up. The shepherd turned and again confronted Spunky Doo. Stop it!

The handler sorted things out, and Spunky Doo returned to us with a 'That was fun!' look on his face. Indeed.

I noticed then, now that Spunky Doo didn't have my full attention, that Winner had gone awol. After a short moment of panic, I realized that he wouldn't leave the area—there was too much going on here. And it was safe. There was no car traffic to speak of, and he was unlikely to get into a fight with another dog. Or a sheep. Most important, there was no way I could pick him out of the crowd. So I figured I'd just wait until everyone went home, and the blue-and-grey shepherd left would be Winn.

Besides, it was the puppies' turn. When the first one took to the field, the big sheep with the horns turned on it and it ran off the field. The second puppy just chased the sheep until it wore itself out. The third puppy was soon joined by a fourth and a fifth—soon every pup had its own sheep to chase. I don't think that's what was supposed to happen, judging by the reaction of a dozen handlers, one of whom was shouting so much, spittle was coming out of his mouth and his face was so red I thought he was going to have a coronary right there and then. All because his dog was having so much fun chasing sheep. (Okay, so I might have to take back my earlier comment....)

At intermission, a video was projected on a large screen set up at the end of the field. We went over to watch. A group of guys calling themselves the Baaa-Studs had trained their dogs to herd black and white sheep on a hillside into the shape of a sheep, like that stupid commercial in which blue and white clad dancers imitate the head of an electric toothbrush. Only here they ended up with a clump of white sheep for the body, a smaller clump of black sheep at the upper right, for the head, complete with two eyes, a single black sheep for each pupil in a circle of white, and four black legs, each a single line of black sheep. Then the camera tech of the group used fast forward and looping videography to make it look like the sheep was walking.

For a second, I thought 'These guys have *way* too much time on their hands.' But hey, I'd rather see them teaching their dogs to herd sheep into a sheep shape than beat each other up on a football field or get together with beer and guns to kill a moose.

Well, come to think of it, I actually don't mind when guys beat each other up on the football field. Or anywhere else. I figure it's a sort of self-selection thing. Darwin at work. Better they beat each other up than the rest of us.

The Baaa-Studs' next act was even better. They'd put blankets of LED lights on the sheep and gotten their dogs to herd the sheep, at night, into what looked like a tennis game: a few stationary sheep, or lit dogs, formed a dotted line down the middle of the hill, then one brightly-lit clump of sheep was herded to each side, they were the players, and then a third dog herded a third clump back and forth from the left clump to the right clump. I bet that third dog, the one herding the 'ball' back and forth over the 'net' had the time of her life! Until it 'missed' the player clump on the left and went 'out of bounds'. How cool is that?

But the coolest was when they sent their dogs, one at a time, racing up the hill in the dark straight into a clump of sheep, which they're typically never allowed to do. When they get there, the sheep disperse, of course. But at each moment of dispersal, the techie turned on the lights the sheep were wearing, so it looked like the dog had triggered a fireworks explosion. Absolutely brilliant whoever thought of that!

And what was really interesting was that the patterns made by the dispersing sheep really did look like the patterns made by fireworks. One even looked like the classic pinwheel you see a lot in photographs of stellar nebula. I wondered whether dispersing schools of fish would make the same patterns. And pollen grains too? Is there some underlying universality to dispersal patterns? Was it fractal? Biological units are, I mused, nothing more than conglomerates of chemical units, we're all atoms…

I didn't see the kitten until it was practically in front of us. It was a cute little fluffy white kitten, tripping over itself like a tumbling marshmallow. I felt, rather than saw, Snookums, who was on the bleacher seat beside me, sink into a crouch. I knew she wasn't going to play with it. Well, not in the sense of puppies and kittens frolicking in a meadow full of flowers and butterflies. But before I could reach out my hand and open my mouth to say 'No!', I heard Chum, Hunk, and Little Miss growl at her. (Spunky Doo didn't get the memo.) They even bared their teeth. Wow. A little over the top, don't you think? Truly, I was surprised. I mean, I know no one wants a kitten to be pounced on, but this is Snookums! Our little sweetheart! And you're baring your teeth at her?

Snookums was also surprised. Her ears went back. She actually cringed.

Until another little white marshmallow tumbled by.

And Snookums flew off the bleacher. Before I could scream to myself 'Why the hell didn't I stuff her into her snuggly after the first one?', Chum flew off the bleacher as well. Because he was bigger and stronger, his trajectory intercepted hers, and he knocked her off course. She rolled out of sight around a corner, which happened to be where the kitten had gone. Chum scrambled after her. Hunk and Little Miss had already left the bleacher as well, barking like crazy. (Again, Spunky Doo didn't get the memo.) (And Kessie just didn't care. No tennis balls were involved.)

By the time I leashed Spunky Doo to the bench and told Kessie to stay, setting her tennis ball beside her to encourage her to do just that, I was a good thirty seconds behind the main event. Would they really hurt her? She *had* violated the terms of the Agreement to which all domesticated animals were bound. Sparrows were okay; budgies were not. Martens were okay; ferrets were not. But how was she to know? She was just a baby. She couldn't read yet.

And actually, martens were *not* okay, I wanted to tell her. They can rip you apart. Much like, I suspected, belatedly, Mama Cat.

Whom I saw as soon as I rounded the corner into one of the tents. Hard to miss, she was hissing at me with her claws extended. Behind her lay one of the little white kittens, near a little puddle. It was moist around the neck. Oh no. I skidded to a stop.

Behind the little white kitten sat Hunk and Little Miss, forming a wall in front of—Chum? Lying down? Had *he* been attacked by Mama? Where was Snookums? I looked around frantically. Hunk shifted slightly and I saw then that Snookums was tucked in between Chum's legs, his left curled protectively around her, his right clamped down on top of her. Okay, good.

Their barks must have been sufficient for my little sensitive soul. She must've dropped the kitten and piddled on the spot. It was limp though. And, as I'd noticed already, moist around the neck. Not a good sign.

I looked back at Snookums and saw, this time, blood on her ear. What else, I was wondered, my heart thumping away. What couldn't I see? How much could've happened in such a short time?

The tent was small, and I couldn't make a wide enough berth around Mama to get to Snookums. Wide enough, that is, not to trigger a homicidal rage on her part. I knew that Mama Bears would tear you apart if you got between it and its cubs. I imagined Mama Cats were the same. And I didn't know where the other little white kitten was.

A little black kitten came out from behind Chum then. Oh no. What have we done? I was afraid there was something really awful behind Chum and Snookums that I didn't want to know about.

Mama Cat hissed, and the little black kitten went into the cage I noticed now, in the corner near the front of the tent. A little white kitten was already inside. The other little white kitten? The little black one curled up beside it on the bunched up towels scattered with little cat toys.

Okay…now what? I thought I should do *something*, but I didn't want to disturb the fragile balance that the dogs seemed to have achieved. And I'm sure everyone but me knew exactly how many kittens there were in the tent. And where exactly they were.

Hunk was quivering slightly. His last encounter with a cat, in the dog park, was not a confidence-builder. But he stood his ground. Beside Little Miss.

Who then decided to break the apparent stale-mate. She leaned forward slightly and nudged the little kitten. Mama Cat hissed. Little Miss stared at her. Had she been paying attention to the shepherds? Or was this a female-to-female thing—was Little Miss apologizing for—

The little kitten moved!

Little Miss stood up, nudged it again, onto its unsteady feet, then stepped back and sat down again beside Hunk.

Mama Cat stepped forward then and picked up the little kitten. She deposited it into the cage. Then sat in front of the open door.

And started grooming herself. Specifically, her private parts.

What did that mean? Were we dismissed? I looked at Little Miss and Hunk. Could we all leave now?

Little Miss stood up and turned to Chum. There was a brief discussion, it seemed to me, and then Little Miss picked up Snookums. Hunk and Chum formed a wall between her and Mama Cat as she walked out of the tent. I thought it best not to intervene.

But as soon as I was out of the tent, I gently took Snookums from Little Miss, thanking her profusely. Once back on our bleacher, I lay Snookums down and checked her thoroughly. Chum, Hunk, and even Little Miss, who until this day had shown no interest whatsoever in Snookums, crowded around, waiting for the verdict.

All I could find was the scratch on her ear, which had by now stopped bleeding. She was lucky. And still cowering. Probably because all three of them were still sending her severe reprimand pheromones. She'd never make that mistake again. She eagerly crawled into her snuggly and didn't come out until we were back in the car. Correction. Until we were back home.

Intermission had ended, and the final event was being announced. Something to determine the winner from among the five finalists. Would be it shedding, which involves separating the sheep into two groups? Or would it be singling, which involves separating just one sheep from the rest? Both were apparently very difficult because sheep really *really* want to stay together. That's why they're called sheep.

No, the five finalist had to herd cats.

I kid you not. The five finalists—had to herd cats.

Okay, the Baaa-Studs must've organized the final event. Only they would've come up with the idea of herding cats. They probably wanted to put little LED lights on them too. On their tails. Swish, swish, in the dark to look like sparklers...

The first finalist was on the field. I couldn't see where the cats were, but I realized now that that's what Mama Cat was doing here.

And the first finalist was off the field. It had refused. Simply refused. To herd cats.

The second finalist was on the field. It started racing around behind three cats. One of whom leapt up a tree. Spunky Doo could help you with that one, I thought to myself. No sooner had the thought formed than— Shit. I got out my cellphone and called the fire department.

The third and fourth finalists were equally unsuccessful.

While the last finalist was trying to stare down a cat—impossible, since cats are notorious for refusing to make eye contact—another australian shepherd ran onto the field. One of the previous finalists? Then another and another and—there were not five, but six, australian shepherds now on the field.

I borrowed my neighbour's binoculars and saw, as I suspected, a bright yellow rope trailing from one of the dogs. Okay, good. I'd found Winn.

Each dog had a cat. More or less. They'd obviously paid attention to the puppies' strategy.

But now what?

It was embarrassing. None of these geniuses could herd even one cat.

And then Hunk sauntered onto the field.

Wait a minute, what? Hunk, in all his sleek muscled doberman grandness, sauntered onto the field. Perhaps emboldened by what had happened in the tent, perhaps still needing to redeem himself for what had happened in the dog park, he—had something in his mouth. Not a kitten, please no. But, you know, that would—

No, not a kitten, I saw, through the binoculars I was refusing to return to my neighbor, but—

One by one the cats fell into line behind him. It was like he was weaving a magic spell with—catnip. He had a catnip toy in his mouth! The feline aphrodisiac.

Way to go, Hunk!

Had he stolen it from the cat cage we'd so eventfully discovered earlier? No, maybe he'd just found it somewhere, there were obviously at least six cats here at the trial. Didn't matter.

He continued walking, catnip in his mouth, toward the pen. All of the cats were following him. *All* of them. Even the one in the tree. The one that used to be in the tree. Spunky Doo, don't ruin Hunk's moment, I pleaded.

He fell in line behind the cats. Spunky Doo, that is.

And Hunk calmly walked *into* the pen, all the cats still following, Spunky Doo bringing up the rear. Then he neatly stepped out of the pen, and a handler appeared from nowhere to close the gate. With Spunky Doo still inside. No doubt, a bonus, as far as Hunk was concerned.

The crowd went wild. Now *that's* how you herd cats!

The Baaa-Studs then made an appearance—I knew it!—and bestowed upon Hunk, with no small ceremony, the beribboned garland that marked him as the winner.

How cool is that.

7

AMBER

About a week later while I was feeding Snookums—and Kessie, since they *had* to get the same stuff—despite their propensity to switch bowls halfway through— Several weeks later while I was feeding Snookums her new Wild Dog kibble, with real salmon—I thought that if she got it in her kibble, she wouldn't feel the need to kill for it—not that she'd be killing any salmon in the field—or at the dog park or even at the beach—but they were out of the kind with real rabbit—I received another interesting call.

"Hello?"

"Hello, is this Brett? The woman who rehabilitates dogs?"

"Well, I—"

"The woman at the shelter told me what you did with Rosie," she said quickly.

"Oh. But I didn't—"

"I'd like you to try to help Amber."

"Amber's a greyhound?" How many abused greyhounds could there be in this town, I wondered.

"No, she's a shepherd cross."

"They race shepherd crosses too?" I was confused.

"No, she's a Search and Rescue dog."

"Oh. Okay, so—"

"And she's severely depressed. That's why—"

Ah.

"Do you know why she's depressed?"

"I do. But knowing why— Would you be willing to come over, meet her—I can explain then." Her voice broke.

"Sure," I said. I was intrigued. And, seeing the already empty dishes, needed to pick up some more Wild Dog kibble.

SO I BUNDLED SNOOKUMS into her snuggly—she barely fit these days, she was growing so quickly—and waited while Kessie decided which of her many tennis balls to take with her. We got into our still very new and shiny metallic red dogmobile and drove over to Amber's house. It was just twenty minutes away.

I pulled into the woman's driveway, told Snookums and Kessie to stay, rolled down the windows for them, then went to the front door. I stepped around a bunch of stuff on the porch—mountain climbing gear?—and knocked on the door.

"Hi, Brett?"

"Yes." I reached out my hand.

"Ange," she said. "Come in. Please."

"I have my two dogs with me," I said. "Do you think it would help if I brought them in? They're both certified therapy dogs."

"Really? That would be—"

“No, I was just kidding.” Was there such a thing? Dogs who were therapists for other dogs? Snookums—the sensitive squiggly part of her, not the ruthless killer part of her—might make a very good therapy dog.

“Oh.” She sounded disappointed. More than disappointed.

“But they’re both sensitive souls,” I lied. “Well, one’s a sensitive soul, the other’s an addict. Can’t go anywhere or do anything without a bright green tennis ball in her mouth.”

She didn’t even smile. What the hell had happened here?

“Okay, sure. Maybe they’ll, I don’t know…” she trailed off, and I went back to my car to get them.

Amber was indeed a shepherd cross. Crossed with an irish setter, I thought. That would explain her striking coloring: german shepherd trimmed in orange. She was absolutely gorgeous. And curled despondently in a corner of the living room. She did not look well.

Ange had a second shepherd, a younger one. Or at least a less depressed one. Specks, a shepherd and border collie cross, I thought, was interested in meeting Kessie and Snookums. Amber was not.

“They’re both SAR dogs,” Ange explained once we were settled in her living room. “‘Search and Rescue,’” she added when she saw my eyebrows raise at the acronym.

“Oh, like when someone gets lost in the forest,” I said.

“Not quite. Amber and Specks are what we call ‘disaster dogs’. They specialize in explosion sites, earthquake sites, that sort of thing. Disaster search-and-rescue requires a somewhat different skill set than wilderness search-and-rescue.”

“I see.” I didn’t, quite, but—

“We worked the school bombing last week.”

I had to confess I hadn’t heard that a school had been bombed. I’d stopped reading or watching the news. Mostly because it wasn’t. News.

"It was awful," Ange said, looking with such heartbreak at Amber, still curled in the corner. "She found every one of the unaccounted kids. And every one of them was—not one survived."

She turned her focus to Specks, rolling on the floor with Snookums. Kessie had given up trying to get either one of us to throw her tennis ball and was tucked beside me on the couch.

"And I knew—these dogs are very empathetic, you're supposed to—every time they find someone who, who hasn't survived, you're supposed to—but everyone who was there was working full out on the rescue, no one had time to play lost-but-alive for Amber. Even if we had someone who could do that, there just wasn't time. For every live find I took the time to stage, another child may have died."

I started to understand.

"And Specks?"

"I'm not sure she's as sensitive as Amber, and in any case, she's just started. Amber's been doing this for a while. I'm afraid this was the straw that broke—that broke her." She pulled a crumpled tissue from her pocket.

I didn't do any 'there, there' shit. Partly because I'm incapable of 'there, there' shit. But mostly because this was something certainly worth crying about. Amber did look broken. She had continued to show no interest at all in—anything.

"She's not coming with us for walks, she's not eating, she's not even interested in her Raggedy." She nodded to a well-worn Raggedy Ann doll on the floor some distance away from her.

"SAR dogs are known for having an over-the-top play impulse," she explained. "A dog that will plow through 10 feet of snow all the way up a mountain just to find its tennis ball and get someone to throw it for her again," she smiled at Kessie, "or dig through two stories of rubble just to play tug-of-war with her Raggedy—"

I wondered if Kessie had missed her calling. Then I considered the irony of a dog who search-and-rescued children taking such delight in tearing a Raggedy Ann apart.

"I've tried everything. We even had her on anti-depressants for a week. But she's—she's barely moved from that spot since we got back. It's like she's given up the will to live."

"And..." I still didn't see where I fit in.

"I'm thinking," she looked at me then, with such hope, "you know how sometimes you just have to get away from it all—spend a week on a beach in Mexico?"

I didn't, but—

"I'm hoping you can be her beach in Mexico. I'm hoping that a total change in her environment, her routine—you have a bunch of dogs that you pick up and do fun stuff with, right?"

"I—" I stopped. Actually, that was a pretty good description of my dog walking job.

"It may be time for her to retire," she gazed sadly at Amber. "I know that. But she's not ready yet. I mean, she shouldn't be ready yet. It takes a long time to train a dog to do this work. Disaster dogs are the SAR elite. And rightly so. Not only do they have to be able to work off-leash, and to find people, they have to be ever so mindful of their environment, they have to be careful not to step on a plank with nails, they have to go up and down half-destroyed stairs— Disaster dogs are champion drug sniffer dogs and champion agility dogs in one."

She must have seen the look on my face.

"No, I'm not—it's not just about the wasted time and effort. Actually, it's not about that at all. It's—Amber's very good at what she does. She has a real knack. It's like—it's like a concert pianist in her twenties getting arthritis. It's not fair. Amber's only four.

"And until now, I've thought—well, it's weird to say that she likes her job, but she—she seems to have understood that what she does is important. She has *wanted* to search and rescue. She likes people. *Especially* kids. She likes finding them. *Rescuing* them. For her, it's *not* all about the reward, the tennis ball, the raggedy—

"I should've have stopped her after the third child. I knew I was putting her at risk. But all the parents were there—and—" she started to cry again.

"Couldn't you have let another dog take over for a while? Give her a break?"

"No, that's just it. Specks did her best. She found two. But—there aren't that many disaster dogs in the province. Or even in the country. We've often travelled four, five hundred miles to get to a site."

Wow. "But wouldn't—I mean, by the time you got there—"

"Oh, they fly us there. She's that good," she added.

I waited a moment. "How many were there?"

"Fifteen," she said very quietly.

Oh God. No wonder Amber was severely depressed. I personally didn't like people. Especially kids. But I could understand that for someone like Amber, finding fifteen dead kids in a row would have been devastating.

SO WE ARRANGED FOR Ange to bring her over the next day. She didn't bring anything else—not her bed, not her dishes, not her Raggedy—nothing that would remind her of her usual life. I was to be her beach in Mexico. I showed Amber to the guest doggy bed. She lay down on it. Didn't bother sniffing it. Didn't circle ten times. Just lay down.

Both Kessie and Snookums could tell something was wrong. They both kept their distance.

But later that evening, Snookums crawled toward Amber's forlorn lump of a body, and tentatively reached out a little paw. Amber didn't care. Snookums moved closer and snuggled up beside her. Amber didn't care.

Day two, Kessie walked up to her and set her tennis ball in front of her. Nothing.

Day three, she still wasn't coming with us on our walks. I didn't want to force her.

In fact, she didn't move at all, except to go out and piddle, until Spunky Doo sat on her. I think it was an accident, but with Spunky Doo, you never know. I'd brought him inside after one of our group walks, desperate for some sort of reaction from Amber.

Day seven, when we got ready for our afternoon adventure—by this time, I was bringing in Chum, Hunk, and Little Miss as well—Amber showed some interest. Okay. Great. I decided that instead of the dog park, or even just a walk around the block, we'd go to the beach. It wasn't Mexico, but there was just sand and water as far as the eye could see. What could be more different from a search and rescue post-bomb or post-earthquake site?

AS SOON AS I let the crew out to do their thing, I saw that Rosie and Charmaine were there, in the distance, doing their thing. And as soon as Rosie was close enough to recognize us, she came sprinting toward me to say 'Hi!' Though on her, a sprint looked more like a relaxed lope. I'd seen her several times since that first day, and every time she looked better. She absolutely beamed as she leaned against me, ducking her head at my hip and swiping her tail back and forth like a windshield wiper.

Charmaine also sprinted toward us. She looked like she was running as fast as she could. Which was, I had to say, very fast indeed.

"Hey," she panted. "I was going to call you. How are you?"

"I'm good, and you?" I accepted Kessie's proffered tennis ball and threw it down the beach. She tore off after it.

"I'm—I'm going to the nationals!" Charmaine all but screamed. And it took the rest of her breath.

"You made the national team?"

"The trials. In Vancouver. And I have Rosie. And you. To thank. She is the best—"

She stopped, and I turned then to see what she was staring at. Rosie, instead of going to Hunk and Little Miss, which was what she usually did after she said 'Hi' to me—I think they have a 'big dog' thing going—had headed to Amber. She must have caught the smell of depression. Perhaps recognized it. She slowly walked toward her, then very gently touched her nose to Amber's nose. Then just as gently, she licked Amber's nose, then her muzzle, her cheeks, and, lastly, her eyes. Then she stood alongside her, seeming to strive for full body contact. If she could have put her four long legs around her and hugged her, I think she would have.

I started to tell Charmaine Amber's story, as we started to walk along the beach, as was our habit, but Chum came up to me at that moment and set his beach ball, his soggy ex-rubber now-sponge ball, onto the sand in front of me. I smiled. We'd worked on this last time we were here. Come out of the water, drop your ball, shake, *then* bring it to me. I threw it into the water, then threw Kessie's tennis ball as far ahead as I could, and then resumed telling Charmaine about Amber.

"Oh god, that must have been awful."

Clearly Charmaine felt differently about kids than I did.

I nodded anyway, and we continued walking. She'd been intending to call in order to ask if I could look after Rosie for the week, a month hence, that she'd be away at the trials. Of course I could. And would. I threw Kessie's ball. I threw Chum's ball.

We continued to catch up on various points of common interest—Rosie, Charmaine's various meets, and whatever else came to mind. I threw Kessie's ball. Hunk had come out of the water, after his initial, vocal, dip, and Little Miss, who always kept a careful eye on him, relaxed. The two of them trotted side by side ahead of us. I threw Kessie's ball. I threw Chum's ball. Snookums was following along beside us, splish splash, plunk, plunk. And Spunky Doo was—I never really know what Spunky Doo is doing. And Amber followed us, listlessly, Rosie at her side. But she was there, following us.

ON THE WAY HOME, we stopped at the pet store. Amber didn't want to come in, but Kessie and Snookums helped me pick out a new quasi-rag doll for her. It was an orange giraffe. Giraffes, I observed, were built for tug-of-war. I hoped Amber liked it.

I CALLED ANGE THE next day to give her an update.

"So I think she's making progress," I summarized. "Would you be willing to give her another week here with us?"

"Yes," the answer came immediately. "You don't mind?"

"Amber's welcome here for as long as she needs, for as long as she wants."

As soon as I said it, we both heard the as-yet-unconsidered possibility.

Ange started crying. It would break her heart, but she'd rather Amber be happy with us than depressed with her.

"You don't know," she wailed. Absolutely wailed. I suspected she wasn't eating either. "They tell us we're not supposed to get too close to them, because they're working dogs, and it's a dangerous job, they put themselves at risk every time— But you can't not—the bond is so strong, from all that training—it has to be. The dog has to trust you, absolutely, when you tell it where to go— You have to be able to read the slightest sign, you have to be able to anticipate— And I let her down— And now, I'm going to lose—"

"Let's not go there yet," I said. If we had to go there, Ange was going to be the one giving up the will to live.

"*I'll* retire," she suddenly blurted. "I'll get rid of all our gear. I'll make it so nothing here will remind her— I'll give the house a makeover. I'll sell the house. Buy another one."

"But what if it's—"

I didn't have to say it. I didn't have to say the as-yet-unsaid possibility.

"I'll cut my hair. I'll change my clothes, I'll start wearing high heels, I'll— I'll use different soap and different shampoo—" she started crying again.

"Wait a minute," I said. "You'd really wear high heels for your dog?"

DAY TEN, WHILE I was in another room, I heard a soft bark. It wasn't Kessie, and Snookums typically didn't bark, stealth hunter that she is. Curious, I went to the other room and saw Amber sitting, staring at Snookums' snuggly which I'd left on the floor. I could see that Snookums had crawled inside. Her little tail was sticking out. And it was wagging.

I correctly deduced that that was how Amber indicated that she'd found someone. It would make sense. I suspect avalanche rescue dogs are trained not to bark at all, lest they bring another mountain of snow down.

I lifted the edge of the snuggly, revealing Snookums who then crawled out. Alive! She squiggled at Amber. Who wagged her tail.

Wagged her tail! I praised Amber, and offered her a treat. She ate it. She ate it! I offered another. Then I gave her the orange giraffe. Not too interested. But, okay, baby steps.

DAY ELEVEN, ANOTHER QUIET bark. Surely Snookums didn't understand, wasn't intentionally—no, Amber was sitting by the couch. Staring intently at the floor. I got down on my hands and knees. Kessie! She'd crawled under to retrieve one of her million tennis balls. And had gotten stuck. I lifted the couch, and Kessie crawled out. Alive! Amber wagged her tail again. I offered a treat. And another. "You," I said to an unstuck Kessie, "have to cut back."

NEXT DAY, I ENCOURAGED both Snookums and Kessie to hide behind the tree in the back yard. "Stay," I said. They obliged. I let Amber out. I didn't give her the 'Search' command. I didn't want to put any pressure on her. Plus, I didn't know what the 'Search' command was. But she started 'working' the yard, and in no time, found them.

Squiggling, tail wagging, and treats ensued. Though just one of the latter for Kessie.

I called Ange to give her the good news.

THEN I CALLED JAN. If anyone was hide-able, Biscuit was. Eminently so. I explained the situation and invited her over.

"We'll be there in an hour," she said with enthusiasm. "No, wait. I can't drive."

Oh, that's right. Her eyesight.

"I don't have a car," she said. "We'll take the bus."

"Nonsense, I'll come get you. Or—"

"Why don't you just come here? Will Amber get in the car?"

"Yes, I think so."

SO, NEXT DAY, KESSIE, Snookums, and Amber and I drove over to visit Biscuit and Jan. I left Kessie and Snookums in the car, thinking they'd ruin the hide-and-seek. Told them they could come in—soon. Made sure the windows were down.

Jan welcomed Amber into her house, introduced her to Biscuit, and then went into the kitchen to rustle up a batch of margaritas. A few minutes later, the four of us were settled into the living room. Jan and Biscuit were on the couch, I was in the chair, Amber lying down beside me.

Jan casually covered Biscuit with the blanket on the couch.

I got up and walked over to the couch, calling Amber to come. She did, wondering why— She pointedly walked to the far end, then sat, and quietly barked.

Yay! Biscuit was uncovered. Alive and well!

A few minutes later, Jan and Biscuit went into the kitchen.

"Brett? Would you like to bring Amber in here?"

I walked into the kitchen with Amber.

"We've been practicing," Jan said, a twinkle in her eye. That's when I noticed the wicker basket on the floor in the corner. The lid had moved. Ever so slightly.

Amber walked around, out of perfunctory curiosity, then—sat and quietly barked.

Yay! Biscuit popped out of the wicker basket, alive!

A short while later, Jan called us into her bedroom. I continued not giving the 'Search' command—partly because I didn't want to put any pressure on Amber, but also because I still didn't know it. I'd forgotten to ask Ange. Amber sniffed the laundry hamper, then walked along the bed, her nose to the floor, then—sat in front of the closet and quietly barked. Jan opened the door and yay! Out popped Biscuit!

"I'm afraid that's the extent of our repertoire," Jan said, leading us back into the living room.

"That was wonderful!" I assured her. And Biscuit. Who already knew he was wonderful.

I went out to the car to get Snookums and Kessie, and the six of us had a delightful visit. Jan and I talked about how Anita Sarkeesian had received such a backlash when she announced she was researching sexism in video games and harassment of women in online gaming environments. Apparently thousands of men took the time to tell her that she was a useless cunt and she was ruining people's fun. She received threats of rape and death, her Wikipedia page was filled with pornographic images, and attempts were made to knock her website offline, hack into her email, and distribute her home address. Someone even made a video game in which the players were invited "beat the bitch up". Jan got us another round of margaritas.

In the meantime, Kessie had obtained permission to use Jan's short hallway as a tennis ball runway, Snookums was delighted meet a dog smaller than her, Biscuit was overjoyed to have so many guests, and Amber was—content.

An hour later, at the door, Jan said, "You tell Ange—it is Ange, right?" I nodded. "You tell her that whenever Amber needs to play hide-and-seek with Biscuit, she should just call me. You'll give her my number?"

"I will," I assured her.

IT WAS THE BIG day. Ange was coming to get Amber. She hoped. Would Amber be happy to see her? Or would the sight of her bring it all back—

As soon as she pulled into our driveway, Amber got up. Amber got up! *And* she went to the door.

I knew Ange would be sitting in her car, unable to move, sobbing, trying to find the courage to face—

I opened the door to put her out of her misery. Ange, not Amber. Amber was not in misery. Amber was happy. Amber was happy! And of course she was. She was being reunited with the love of her life.

"This is Amber's," I said to Ange a few minutes later, giving her Amber's orange giraffe. It was in two pieces. Three actually. I just didn't know where the head was.

Ange understood immediately—not that I didn't know where the head was, but that the lack of a head meant that a tug-of-war had occurred—and she started crying again.

A MONTH LATER, WHEN I called Ange for an update, she told me that Amber had returned to work, but had apparently decided to specialize in rescuing only dogs, leaving it up to Specks to find the people. Which I thought was just fine.

8

COOKIE

The next day, we went to the dog park and did two circuits of the larger path. Toby the Turtle was waiting for us when we got back to our car. Well, his person, I couldn't remember her name, and two guys were waiting for us when we got back to our car. Toby was actually just standing there.

And he wasn't actually a turtle. He was a bulldog in a turtle costume. His person had discovered that whenever he wore the costume, his shyness disappeared. I kid you not. Normally, when someone came to the door, she'd explained one day, when I'd asked what was up with the costume, Toby would take off and hide. When they were in the family room watching tv, he'd act like a wallflower at the prom unless they gave over-the-top encouragement to him to come join them. At dinner time, he'd hang back until their gerbil was finished eating before stepping up to his dish.

Then one day, when she answered the door, she accidently dropped her guest's jacket on him at just the moment he was running away. And he stopped. Turned. And faced the visitor. Even wagged his stubby little tail.

"So why a turtle costume?" I'd asked.

"It's all I had on hand," she'd said. "Jimmy, my four-year-old, had worn it the previous Hallowe'en. He was into the Ninja Turtles. And it fit Toby perfectly."

It did indeed. And every time I saw Toby trot through the dog park with bulldog confidence and authority, in his turtle costume, I thought of men, in their suitcoats.

ANYWAY. WHEN WE GOT back to the car, Toby was there, with his person and two guys.

"Hi," she said. "Remember me? Meredith?"

"Right, hi," I said, then bent down to greet Toby. He was surrounded by similar greetings—well, not exactly similar—from Spunky Doo, Chum, Hunk, Little Miss, Kessie, and Snookums.

"This is my husband Michael, and his brother Daniel."

"Mike," Michael said, reaching out to shake my hand as I stood up.

"Dan" followed suit.

"This might seem like a weird question," Meredith said, "but," she looked around nervously, "do you consider yourself a law-abiding person?"

"Depends on the law," I replied.

They looked at each other, conferring, looked at my canine crew for some reason, then seemed to reach an agreement.

"We're planning something," Michael—Mike took over, "and we're wondering if you'd be interested in helping."

"Depends..." I replied, and put the dogs into the dogmobile. This sounded like it was going to become a conversation that needed my full attention.

They proceeded to tell me that they were part of a larger group that was planning to do a puppy mill rescue that night. At the last minute, one of their drivers had to drop out, and they needed a replacement vehicle. Specifically, a replacement vehicle large enough to hold several cages. Ah.

"We'll do the actual B & E," Mike lowered his voice. "All we need you to do is let us load some of the puppies into your vehicle."

"And then?"

"You follow us back to our place," Meredith said. "We're set up to take it from there."

I thought about it. I'd still be implicated. If they got caught. I had no idea what that would mean in the long run, but what would happen to Kessie and Snookums if I had to spend the night in jail? I could call Jan. I could take them to her place. Just in case. She'd understand.

Or I could just take off as soon as I saw the police arrive.

"Where is it?" I asked.

"It's—"

"We'd rather you didn't know," Mike interrupted her, "at this point in time. It's out of the city though. We'll hear the sirens in advance." He'd read my thought.

"And you've done the research?"

"No security on the premises," Dan said. "Not even an alarm system."

"And it *is* a puppy mill? I mean, the conditions—"

"—are awful," Meredith confirmed.

"Okay," I said. I didn't really know these people, but what could go wrong?

"Okay, good," Mike said, nodding.

“Thanks,” Meredith added.

“So…”

“So meet us back here at eight o’clock.”

“Okay.”

I retrieved Toby’s turtle head from Spunky Doo’s mouth and gave it back to him, at which point he stopped cowering behind Meredith.

AS SOON AS I got home, I called Jan and explained the situation.

“Yes, by all means,” she said, “bring Kessie and Snookums over. They can stay the night if need be.”

“Thank you!”

“Take my number in case you need bail.”

“Okay, thanks.”

“Cover up your licence plate,” she advised. “And wear dark clothing. Long pants, long shirt. Soak a bandana in lemon juice or vinegar and take it in a baggie. When you get there, put it on, over your nose and mouth. In case you’re tear gassed. Also take a bottle of water. If it gets in your eyes, flush them with the water. Do you have any pepper spray?”

“I have a flashlight,” I said.

SO I PREPARED MY vehicle, covering the licence plate as Jan recommended. Well, partly. I was sure that doing so was illegal, so I tried to make it just accidentally dirty, too dirty to make out the numbers. I put the back seat down and covered the floor with newspapers. I threw in a couple towels and blankets. Don’t quite know why. I decided to forego the tear gas preparations. But I did remember to check the batteries in my flashlight.

At eight o'clock, I was back at the dog park. Two minutes later, a minivan pulled into the lot. Meredith waved from the back seat. Dan got out of the passenger seat and came over to my door.

"I'll drive," he said to me.

"What?"

"I'll drive," he repeated. "Your car."

"Why should you drive? My car."

He acted as if I'd turned down a polite offer. What I'd done, instead, was call him out on a stupid asshole move to be, literally, in the driver's seat. Typical male.

"One, it's my car," I said to him. "Two, I'm perfectly capable of driving. My car. Three, I'm a woman. Women are better drivers than men."

He snorted.

"*You're* the ones paying the higher premiums. Why do you think that is?"

That stopped him.

"Guess you'll just have to ride along with Meredith and Mike, in the back seat," I rubbed it in, having seen Meredith climb into the passenger seat. Though why riding in the back seat should be so emasculating, so subordinating, I have no idea. But I do know men would rather not go, anywhere, than get there by riding in the back seat. They have enough trouble riding in the passenger seat. Unless, of course, the back seat is in a limo and they're being chauffeured.

"Bitch," I heard him say as he walked away.

"Asshole," he heard me say. And if it weren't for the puppies, he would have seen me drive away.

SO I FOLLOWED THEIR minivan, and half an hour later, we were parked in front of an abandoned warehouse. I turned off my ignition and waited. After a few minutes, I saw Mike and Dan exit their vehicle. Meredith slid over into the driver's seat. The two men were wearing camouflage. Matching full-body outfits. They had night vision goggles, a crow bar, heavy duty bolt cutters, a grappling hook and a long length of rope, and a bunch of other stuff straight out of *Mission Impossible*. I checked my flashlight.

They approached my car and gestured for me to roll down my window.

"What, no bulletproof vests?" I asked.

They ignored my question.

"Wait here," Mike commanded.

And I suddenly had a vision of a cross-stitched wall hanging that said not 'Home, Sweet Home,' but 'Wait Here.'

Well fuck that, I thought to myself, thinking of a wall hanging with *that* cross-stitched on it. Then I thought of Kessie and Snookums.

"I'll wait here," I told him. As if it was my idea and I was insisting on it. He gave me a weird look.

Clueless, I thought. Why do men continue to be so clueless about gender politics? So *utterly* clueless. I wondered if cross-stitching came in italics.

AS SOON AS I saw them come out of the building with a cage, I got out and opened the back door of my car.

"We've got it covered," Dan said dismissively.

"There was just the one cage," Mike explained, sounding disappointed, as they loaded the cage into their minivan. "Our intel was incorrect."

Our intel? And why the disapp—ah. On top of that, there were only three puppies in the cage. Would the insults to their manhood never stop?

They closed the back doors of their vehicle and drove off.

Well, I thought, since I was here, I may as well take a look around. Morbid curiosity, I suppose. I wanted to know what a puppy mill looked like exactly.

A few minutes later, standing in the middle of an airless garage-like space, thick with the stench of shit and vomit, I decided I didn't need to know, exactly.

But as I turned to leave, a slight movement in the beam of my flashlight caught my eye. Another cage. More puppies?

I went closer to investigate. No, not more puppies. Just one. And not a puppy. She was small, yes, but she not a puppy. She was thin and lumpy. Her black coat was matted with feces, except where it had fallen out in chunks. At those places, I could see red sores. And her bum was—this was the mother. Oh god, this must be one of the moms of all those puppies. I could see her several teats, red, swollen, and, well, yukky— How long had she been caged and forced to be pregnant again and again? Perhaps that's all she'd ever known. She was just a baby-making machine for whoever—

Right, I thought, save the puppies, they're all cute and innocent, but no one thinks of the mom. Just like all those pro-life morons, all gushy about the babies, as if their lives are more important than the women in whose bodies they grow without their consent.

I started talking to dog, softly, calmly, then opened the cage door. She was too weak, too ill, to be aggressive. She was beyond caring, and didn't even try to come to me, should she be thinking, against all odds, that I might be there to help her. I reached and gently tugged her toward me. She felt—stuck. Oh god, some of the oozing pus must have dried to the wire—

"I'll be back," I told her, then ran out to my car to get the gallon jug of water I kept in one of the step/storage/pawrest boxes. I also grabbed the blanket I'd brought.

When I returned, I poured a bit of water onto the stuck part. She twisted her head back and tried to drink it. Right. Stupid me. Of course. I poured some water into my hand and offered it to her. She lapped it up needily. I poured another handful. And another. And another.

Then I tried again to loosen the crusted bit from the wire, lifting her as I freed her, half-inch by half-inch onto the blanket.

And then I felt something squirm under her. I yanked my hand back. What the— Couldn't be a puppy, could it? No, I reflected, it was—eew. I have trouble with anything that doesn't have fur, feathers, or legs. And that includes worms and maggots and whatever the hell might be crawling on—feasting on—an open wound. And me without any gloves.

I tried to drown or flush away the whatever the hell with half the gallon at once, and quickened my efforts.

"I'm sorry," I said a few seconds later, sure I had just broken open something that may have been partly healed.

But a few seconds after that, I was able to gather her into the blanket. I folded it and folded it again, then set her by the door. I then walked through the building, covering every inch, to make sure there weren't any more mom dogs, abandoned now that they were useless. She was the only one. I carried her out to my car and set her in the back, wishing I had some duct tape. If anything should crawl out into my car—

Lucky for me, and the poor little dog, this was the one day of the week the vet was open in the evenings, so I broke every speed limit driving to it. After all, my licence plate was illegible.

"I DON'T WANT TO know how you came to find her, do I," Dr. Vail said, as she unfolded the bundle I'd set on her stainless steel examination table.

"No," I said to her. "I found her on the street. Well, not actually on the *street* street. On the sidewalk. Beside the street." I was so not a liar.

"Oh, god," she gasped once the dog was completely unbundled, more dead than alive, it seemed to me then, except for the eyes indicating consciousness. She quickly recovered her composure and looked up at me. "If you happen to find any more, on the sidewalk, you bring them in."

I nodded.

She gloved her hands, then began to run them gently along the dog's ribs.

"You might want to start by turning her over," I suggested.

She quickly finished her preliminary examination to ensure there were no broken bones, then carefully turned the little dog over per my suggestion. I gagged.

After flushing the area with a sterile saline solution, Dr. Vail picked off the remaining maggots with tweezers. Then simply resumed her examination.

"Her last litter must have been a very difficult one," she said, having gently moved the tail and lifted a leg.

"And she has severe mastitis," she'd parted the matted hair along her torso.

She turned to her cabinet then, prepared a syringe, and made the injection. "For the pain she must be in," she simply said.

"Eyes and ears," she continued her examination, "so-so."

She eased open the mouth. The little dog offered no resistance whatsoever. "Looks like a few of her teeth are rotten."

She sighed then, hands resting on the table on either side of the sodden mess of a creature in front of her, as she gave me her summary. "It looks like she's spent her entire life, which I put at around three years, caged, and pregnant or nursing."

"So, is she—will she—"

"We'll give her a good soak, clean her up, give her a haircut, some fluids, some food, a full set of shots, some antibiotics, then we'll see. If she's strong enough, I'll repair the damage—give her a hysterectomy probably. Perhaps also a mastectomy. And I'll take care of those teeth while she's under."

I nodded, and turned to leave. She turned back to the forsaken little dog. Forsaken until now.

"Oh, Brett," she said, with all the calmness of someone who would really like to have an assault weapon in their hands, "if you should happen to remember the name of the street, you might want to mention it to my receptionist."

I LEFT THE LITTLE dog there, and went to Jan's to pick up Snookums and Kessie. I snuggled them both as I told her what had happened.

"Well, I'm sure you'll find a good home for her."

"Actually, I was thinking—"

It took her just a moment. "Oh no, I—"

"Hear me out," I said. "You're probably thinking you can barely deal with Biscuit, but if you had another dog—and she's very small, like Biscuit— she's a pekinese, or a pomeranian, one of the frou-frou breeds—"

"Frou-frou?"

"That's what I call them," I said. "Anyway, they could be each other's playmate. And on days you couldn't take Biscuit for a walk, you could just let the two of them outside." I nodded to her patio door. "That opens onto a fenced-in common area, right?"

"Yes," she replied, considering what I'd said. "But I can't afford—"

"I can," I said. "I'll take care of the money, you take care of the love and affection."

She thought about it, then sighed. "I am starting to have more bad days than good," she confessed, "and I do feel awful about Biscuit not getting a walk on the bad days."

And, I thought, when you go to the hospital and don't come back, Biscuit won't be left all alone this time. He'll have Cookie—which is what I'd already named the little dog.

LATE THE NEXT DAY, Dr. Vail called to report that Cookie had rallied sufficiently to indicate that she would survive surgery. I gave the go-ahead.

A few days after that, she called to report that Cookie was in recovery and all was well.

"Under normal circumstances," Dr. Vail said, "you could pick her up the day after tomorrow, but if it's all the same to you, I'd like to keep her under observation for the week."

"That would be fine," I replied, thinking it best, given Jan and Biscuit.

I HAD PLANNED TO go to the pet store myself—well, with Snookums and Kessie, of course—to buy whatever Cookie would need, but then thought that Jan probably didn't get out much, so I asked if she and Biscuit wanted to come along. They did indeed.

"What's the little dog's name?" Jan asked on the way.

"I don't think she has one," I said. "You could name her Cookie," I suggested.

"No, I think she needs something with more dignity," she said. "After all she's been through."

I didn't disagree..

"Margaret," Jan pronounced just as we pulled into the parking lot. "I'm going to call her Margaret Sanger."

I—

"Cookie, for short," she added, grinning out the window.

I smiled.

We picked out a collar, leash, and harness. Regarding the latter, Biscuit and Snookums obliged by helping us figure out the right size. It seemed to me that Cookie was roughly Biscuit's height and length, but was closer to Snookums in girth. We didn't know if she would be into chase toys, tug-of-war toys, chew toys, snuggle toys, or squeak toys. So we got one of each. For Cookie. Biscuit, Kessie, and Snookums somehow walked away with a few new toys as well.

Biscuit chose a purple soft ring toy which he wore over his head around his neck. Don't quite know why.

Kessie chose, of course, a bag of tennis balls. Just a three-pack. An emergency-size pack. It would fit in the step/storage/ pawrest box in the car. In case she ever forgot her ball. Right. Actually, that was a good idea, now that I thought of it. Could happen.

Snookums chose not a squeaky mouse, but a squeaky gorilla. Clearly she was upping her game. And actually, it didn't so much as squeak, as scream. Screams were apparently far more exciting than squeaks. Good thing we didn't live in the jungle.

We got Cookie several different kinds of treats as well: cheese, beef, liver, and salmon. I said I'd get a bag of kibble when I picked her up from the vet, suspecting that Dr. Vail would put her on some special recovery diet for a while, something full of supplements or what have you.

And then we picked out a bed. I gravitated toward the cheaper ones, because in my experience, no dog ever slept in its own bed anyway—or, rather, its bed was my bed—which was, for that reason, a mattress on the floor—but I saw Jan pause at the more expensive plush ones. And then I realized that probably what with her having a real bed and all, and Biscuit being a chihuahua, Cookie probably would be sleeping in her own doggy bed.

"What colour?" I said as I joined her beside the more expensive plush ones.

"Are you sure?" she asked. "They're considerably more expensive," she said, squeezing the oh-so-thick foam on a lime green one, while she glanced at the cheaper ones.

"Absolutely. Cookie has spent her entire life sleeping in a wire cage on a concrete floor. She's getting the softest, plushest bed we can buy. Extra pillows too, if you like."

A FEW DAYS LATER, Cookie was ready. Jan and Biscuit were ready. And Snookums and Kessie were always ready.

I paid the bill without looking—just handed over my credit card—and Dr. Vail brought her out herself.

Ooh-la-la! Cookie was a cute little fluffy black frou-frou. With bright little button eyes. What a difference the proper care had made!

"She's healed well," Dr. Vail said. "Just getting her out of there—she's healed well," she repeated, her eyes starting to tear.

I nodded.

"Our co-op student has been walking her around a bit. Mostly inside, but she took her outside a couple days ago for the first time. She likes laying on the grass," she started to tear again, "in the sun."

I nodded again.

"No kibble for a couple weeks yet. Canned food only. She's going to someone who understands what she's been through?"

"Yes," I assured her.

"There's no telling what psychological issues she might have. Fear issues certainly. Trust issues probably. Give her time. She'll come through, I think. She's a smart little cookie. Have you named her yet?"

THE DAY AFTER I'D delivered her to Jan, I called for an update.

Cookie wasn't housetrained, of course. Since she'd never had a house. But Biscuit was helping out and once she realized she didn't have to poop in her own bed, so to speak, she didn't.

In fact, apparently Biscuit hardly left her side. He must have sensed Cookie's vulnerability, her confusion—everything was new, it must be overwhelming.

"We're taking it slow," Jan said. "I have to remember Cookie's only ever seen the inside of that damned puppy mill and the vet's office. She's never seen furniture before, or carpet, or someone's shoes sitting at the door. Or a door, for that matter.

"And at first," Jan continued, "I thought she was lame. Her back legs don't seem to work independently very well, she does a sort of three-legged hop. But then I realized she's probably just weak. Like those baby veals kept in cages too small to even turn around, so their flesh stays tender."

"I don't think they're called baby veals."

"Of course, they're not. I just can't think of the word, and can't be bothered to struggle with my memory. You know what I mean."

"I do."

"Speaking of doors, she has trouble with the step down out the patio door, so I put an old board there to make a ramp.

"And oh, Brett," she continued, enthusiastically, "I wish you'd been here to see her go out onto the little yard for the first time. She just stood there. And then she took a couple steps, squatted, and piddled. Then she just sighed like—"

"Like heaven was having a patch of grass to piddle on?"

"Yes! And then she went right to the patch of sun and lay down. Spent the whole afternoon out there, moving from one patch to the next, staying in the warmth of the sun.

"I've cut a hole in the screen, and I'm leaving the door open, so she can go outside whenever she wants.

"And music! She likes Vivaldi. I moved her bed to the sweet spot between the two speakers, and she lay there listening, really listening, to the entire *Four Seasons*.

"And Brian Eno. You were right!"

I'd told her about Brian Eno's ambient music. All dogs love it. It blisses them right out.

"After dinner last night, the three of us fell asleep on the couch with *Ambient 1* on the stereo."

Overwhelmed, yes, but safe. Cookie must have realized that. There would be no more thirst, no more hunger—no more pain.

There would be grass, and sun, and—music.

9

BO

Sometimes when you miss a turn, good things happen. After one of our dog park afternoons, on my way to drop off Little Miss, then Hunk, then Spunky Doo—Chum was still walking home on his own—I missed a turn near Little Miss' house and ended up passing by a large field I hadn't known was there. A couple kids were playing frisbee with their dog. The dog—looked like a border collie—was very good.

So I pulled over, and we all decided to get out and sit in the bleachers to watch for a bit. The young man threw the frisbee five or six times for every time he let the young woman do so. Typical, I thought.

After a few minutes, the young woman came trotting over to us. She was small and waify, but had an I'm-going-to-dress-this-way-and-I-don't-care-what-anyone-thinks thing going for her. Which, since I'd put her at thirteen, maybe fourteen, was impressive.

"Hi!" she said to me.

"Hi!" I said back.

"Do any of your dogs play frisbee?" To the point. I liked that in a person.

"I don't know."

She looked at me like I was an idiot. I liked that in a person.

"Only these two are mine," I explained, putting my hands on Kessie and Snookums, tucked beside me on my left and right, respectively. "Hunk, Little Miss, Chum, and—" I nodded to each in turn, all sitting on the bench behind me, "shit—" I stood up. Where was Spunky Doo?

"He's under there," she pointed calmly to the end of the bleachers. He was stuck again.

"Ah. Thanks. That's Spunky Doo." We watched as he tried to extricate himself from his stuckness.

"I'm Sky," she said, holding out her hand.

"Brett," I said, shaking her hand.

"So you're just their dogwalker or something?"

"Yeah. Something..." I trailed off as I went to help Spunky Doo. If only you didn't have those extra legs, huh.

"There's a competition in a couple weeks," she said, when I'd returned to my seat, between Kessie and Snookums, they made sure of that, "and I wanted to enter with Rice," she nodded to the border collie who had continued to make amazing catches, "but a dog can be entered only once, and my brother's entering with her."

"They're very good."

She nodded.

"Do you think he'd be any good?" She nodded to Hunk. Of the six of us—well, seven of us—he did look the most athletic.

"Why don't we see?"

“Yeah?” It was almost like she dared not get her hopes up. I got the impression Sky was a serious kid, and passionate, just not overly expressive. Maybe her brother mocked her heart whenever it was on her sleeve.

“Yeah!”

She led a willing Hunk, totally unafraid of his doberman-ness, to a spot about fifty feet from the bleachers. She talked to him a bit, then made a few fake throw starts, to get him to understand he was to go after the frisbee (though I suspected the architect guy who owned him had actually thrown one for him a few times—it’d be the kind of thing he’d do) (on a summer’s day in the park, in a lame attempt to attract a woman) (‘Ooh, look, there’s a man throwing a frisbee to a big dog, how impressive, how unusual, he must have all the qualities I want in a man!’).

And then she let it rip. Hunk ran after it, keeping his eye on it, following its path in the air, and then when he was more or less in the right position, he turned, crouched, and leapt for it. He went exactly two inches into the air. Fell short by a couple feet.

“Not a lot of vertical lift,” Sky called out to me, dryly.

“Try again,” I said, seeing that Hunk had returned the frisbee to her.

She threw it again. Same result. He was fast enough, he was coordinated enough, he just had no spring at all.

“What about the lab?” Sky suggested, coming over to me. Hunk retired to his seat beside Little Miss.

“Okay, Chum, you’re up.” I walked with him onto the field, since he didn’t seem quite as willing, or perhaps as familiar with the whole endeavour, as Hunk had been. Which was a bit odd, I thought, given his fondness for chasing after his beach ball into the water.

“Why not just throw it to him from close-up,” I suggested. “Let’s see how he jumps first, before we test his running-for-it ability.”

"Okay."

Sky threw the frisbee straight at him. He ran away from it. Straight back to the bleachers.

Okay, that was a surprise.

"The little one with the ball in her mouth?"

"Maybe," I said. But I doubted it.

"Come 'ere, Kessie!" She trotted straight to me. With great anticipation.

I took the ball out of her mouth with my left hand.

"Let me throw it," I said to Sky, reaching out for the frisbee with my right hand. "That might help get her started."

"Okay, ready?" I asked Kessie. She didn't look ready.

"Ready?" I asked again, crouching as if to remind her what 'ready' looked like, then threw the frisbee.

She watched it fly. Then pointedly stared at my left hand, then crouched, ready.

"Yeah, I didn't think so," I said. "She's a ball dog." I threw her ball, since she was very ready, and we both watched her race after it, scooping it up at sprint speed without missing a step.

Me next! My turn! Snookums had come onto the field and was standing between us. Ready! She crouched, eyes straight ahead.

Sky threw the frisbee for her, adjusting the speed and distance just slightly to take into account her puppy-ness. Snookums took off. Wow. I was amazed. She kept up with it, she totally tracked it in the air overhead as she ran, she timed her turn perfectly, got herself into position, let it fall to the ground, pounced on it, shook it as hard as she could, then ran with it to the nearest bush and buried it for later.

"Sorry about that," I said, starting toward the bush.

"It's okay," Sky replied, grinning just a bit. "I have another one." She sprinted back where her brother was still practicing with Rice, and still ignoring her, then quickly returned with another frisbee.

Okay, Spunky Doo's turn. He had a lot of spring to his step, maybe he'd—surprise us.

The first two throws hit him in the head. To be fair, he was facing the wrong way for the first one. Sky threw the frisbee again. This time, it hit him in the chest. But at least he was airborne when that happened. Ten throws later, he caught it. With his paws, but hey. Unfortunately, he used all four to hang onto it, and had nothing to land on.

Oof.

That had to have hurt. I ran toward him. "Stay! Wait!" You're not supposed to move injured people. "Remain immobile!"

He was dazed, but when I ran my hands along his body, nothing seemed broken. Like the drunks who fall out of second storey windows, I thought. Maybe he just got the wind knocked out of him. I helped him get up and walked him slowly back to the bleachers.

"He's okay?" Sky asked, concerned.

"I think so," I replied.

"So," she said, "the poodle?"

"She's all we've got left."

Little Miss had been watching. She'd been watching Rice. And she was ready. Oh so ready. As soon as Sky let the frisbee fly, she ran, flat out, didn't even need to look up, she knew exactly where it was, she turned and leapt, her body arching, her neck extending, her mouth opening—she caught it, perfectly, and landed. Safely.

"Wow," we both said.

"Again," I said excitedly.

Sky threw again. Little Miss made another spectacular catch. Hunk howled his applause.

Ten more throws. Little Miss didn't miss a one.

"So," I said, when Sky and I were back at the bleachers, "when is this competition?" Little Miss I'm-too-sexy-for-Milan, a Frisbee

Dog. Who'd've thought?

"Two weeks from now. We'd have to practice though," Sky allowed herself to get excited. A little. "In the Toss-and-Fetch category, you have 60 seconds to make as many throws as possible. The dogs are awarded points based on how far they go to make the catch. If they catch it in the air, that's extra.

"Then there's the Freestyle. But we don't have enough time to get ready for that." Was that disappointment? I think it was.

"Is that when the person has more than one frisbee, and there's all those fancy moves and choreography?"

"Yeah."

I thought a minute. "Do you *want* to enter that category as well?"

"Yeah," she admitted.

"Okay, so what if we met here every day after school for the next two weeks?"

"Really?"

"Would that give you time to get something together, do you think?"

"Maybe." Again, enthusiasm, but so—constrained.

"Well, then, let's do it!"

"Okay!" she smiled, a bit nervously. But she smiled.

BACK AT THE CAR, Spunky Doo refused to jump into the trunk. Well, it wasn't really a trunk, but we all liked to call it that when we put Spunky Doo there.

Hm. Maybe he *did* hurt himself, I thought. I was going to give him a boost, but he wouldn't even put his paws up.

So I got Hunk to move over, pulled out the step box, and put it by the back door. Spunky Doo carefully stepped up and in, but then didn't lay down. Yeah, something wrong. Something seriously wrong. Shit. And all this time—I wasn't paying attention—

I drove straight to the vet.

Once, there, Spunky Doo wouldn't come out. Or couldn't come out.

I went in to explain the situation to Dr. Vail.

"Amanda, get the ramp," she said to her assistant.

Cool. They had a ramp they just put up against the back of the car. We led Spunky Doo down the ramp and straight into one of the examination rooms.

"What happened here?" she asked, noting a bump at the back of his head.

"Hit in the head by a frisbee."

"And here?" she lifted a swollen lip.

"Hit in the head by a frisbee."

She glared at me.

"That's how—he did eventually manage to catch one, but had a hard landing."

"How hard, exactly?"

"He came down completely on his side," I confessed. "He was holding the frisbee with all four paws."

"Interesting technique," she murmured as she proceeded to feel along his ribs.

"It's possible he broke a rib," she said, "or maybe just bruised it. An x-ray could tell us which, but the treatment is the same...have you noticed any trouble breathing?"

"No. I don't think so." I wasn't paying attention! Spunky Doo, I'm so sorry!

She walked around to his other side again. Palpated every inch of his torso. "No signs of internal bleeding."

"And he does seem to be breathing okay," I was watching. Now.

"Okay, I'm just going to tape up his ribs a bit," she said, "and do something about those other contusions."

She turned to her cabinet to get what she needed, then began to work on Spunky Doo.

"How's the little—"

"Cookie's doing wonderfully," I said. "In fact, I had had to make an emergency delivery of toilet paper."

She looked up from Spunky Doo.

"Apparently she's getting into *everything*," I smiled, remembering that Jan had practically wailed, describing the mess she'd made. "Can't get enough of the world. Now that she has the chance." She must have been so bored. For so very long.

"Or it could just be she's going through the terrible twos," she said. "She probably missed her entire puppyhood."

I hadn't thought of that. I made a note to tell Jan. That it could just be a phase.

Dr. Vail resumed working on Spunky Doo. By the time she was through, he looked a little like the dog in that Rockwell painting. And he knew it.

NEXT DAY, AND ALL the next days after that for two weeks, I was at the field at four o'clock with Little Miss. And, of course, Kessie, Snookums, Chum, and Hunk. Spunky Doo was on doctor's orders to remain immobile. Right.

I hauled out the two gallons of water I'd brought and a big dish, and set it up at our spot at the bleachers. Sky, who was already there, added the gallon she'd brought. I smiled.

I saw that she'd also brought half a dozen new frisbees.

"I bought these yesterday. They're real dog frisbees. Well, flying discs. They're not actually frisbees. Ordinary frisbees can hurt the dog if it doesn't catch them right."

I thought of Spunky Doo. "Good idea. How much do I owe you?"

"Oh you don't—"

But I saw that I did. "I insist."

"Okay."

"Only thing is," she said, tucking the money into her knapsack, "they throw different. So I sort of have to learn all over again how to throw a frisbee. A flying disc."

I nodded.

She and Little Miss headed off to the middle of the field and started practicing.

I watched them. Sometimes Sky made a mistake. She threw it too high for Little Miss to catch, or so low she didn't even have to leave the ground. Sometimes she threw it too far and Little Miss never got there at all. Or not far enough and Little Miss ended up being there too early then just standing there. And sometimes Little Miss made a mistake. She took her eyes off the disc and missed. Or, more often, she turned to jump too soon and then couldn't jump high enough. I could see that the sport required a great deal of skill and timing and rapport. Sky had to develop a good sense of Little Miss' speed and distance, and then make sure the disc was at the right place at the right time—and at the right height.

After a short while, she led Little Miss over to me. "You're supposed to give the dog a break every fifteen minutes."

I got the impression she had spent the previous night reading all about disc dog training. "Okay, good." I was worried about over-use injuries.

"But I'm gonna keep practicing, okay? You'll watch her?"

"I will."

And Little Miss watched her. We both did. She was very good. And getting better.

"Little Miss—that's a stupid name," Sky said when they came over to the bleachers for their second break.

I agreed.

"And it's too long. When we're on the field—"

"Her name's *actually* Little Miss Bo Peep," I said.

"Seriously?"

"Seriously."

She sat down beside me and took a long drink from a water bottle she'd also brought. For herself. "Do you think she'd respond to 'Bo'?"

"She might."

Sky started calling Little Miss 'Bo'. And she did indeed respond.

When Sky decided to join us for the third break, I told her about Little Miss. About the fashion show and how it was weeks before she was allowed to join us again. About the itsy-bitsy-polka-dotted bikini.

"So why do you think her person is letting her do *this*?"

"Well, she's not, exactly," I said. "I told her we were going to cheerleading practice."

Sky burst out in a laugh. It was the first time I'd heard her laugh.

THE FIRST COUPLE DAYS—after increasingly enthusiastic meet-and-greets between Sky and Little Miss—were spent focusing on the throws and catches. The next couple days were focused on the bringing-it-back part. By the end of the first week, they were ready for the Toss-and-Fetch.

ON THE FIRST DAY of the second week, during Little—Bo's first break, Sky set out several pieces of newspaper in a very large circle around her and repeatedly tried to throw the disc so it landed right on each piece of paper. No, I realized after a while, she was trying to aim the disc about six or seven feet above each piece of paper. Each throw was different. Forehand, back hand, right hand, left hand, from under her leg, from behind her back. Little Miss watched carefully.

After her break was over, Sky came over to join us.

"I've figured out what to do for the Freestyle," she explained when she came to join us after a while. "We're going to do, like, a spoke dance. I'm going to stand in the middle of a circle, and throw the disc out to a certain point. Bo's going to run and catch it, then return to me in the center, drop it, then run back out to the next point on the circle for the next catch."

Ah. I nodded.

"Normally the dog's doing all sorts of tricks, but—"

"We don't have time to teach her any tricks," I said. "To compensate, *you're* doing the tricks. Clever."

She smiled.

"Do you think she'll understand what I want her to do?"

"I think so. Eventually."

She understood by the end of the first day.

AND BY THE END of the next day, it was clear we needed to spruce up the spoke dance.

"I have an idea," I said. "Why not have Little—Bo alternate high and low catches? That would make your spoke dance a little more interesting."

Sky thought about that. "I could say 'High' and 'Low' before each throw, so she'd know what to expect."

"And in the Freestyle, they don't really get marks for the height, right? So you can make the low ones, like, just knee high and the high ones spectacular. For the contrast."

"Yeah!" She liked the idea.

I watched them work on it that way.

"You know what?" I said to Sky on their first break. "It's looking like a merry-go-round! You know, like the horses going around up and down!"

"It does? Yeah, I guess it does. We can call it that. The merry-go-round! Instead of the spoke dance."

WE GOT TO THE field a few minutes before Sky the next day, so I took the opportunity to do some refresher training. I gathered all the dogs around me and said 'High' and jumped up, encouraging them all to jump up with me. They did so. Then I said 'Low' and squatted down, encouraging them all to get down. They did so. I said 'High' again and we all jumped up, then I said 'Low' again and we all squatted down. What fun.

By the end of their first break, it was clear the merry-go-round still wasn't exciting enough. Even with the 'High' and 'Low' which Little Miss—Bo—everyone—had mastered. (I doubted the judges would give extra marks for our sideline performance.)

"What kinds of things have other dogs and their people done?" I asked Sky.

"Well, that's just it. Usually the dog jumps onto the person's back and takes off from there, or weaves in and out between the person's legs—"

"But you and Little Miss can't do those tricks. Because of your relative size."

She nodded.

So we tried to think of other tricks. Easy tricks Little Miss could learn in a couple days.

"What if you got her to lay down when she brought it back to you," I said, "and *you* jumped over *her*? Make into a funny reversal.

And then for her to take off from lying down, that'd be impressive, right? And different?"

We gave it a shot. But there was no way Little Miss was going to lay down. On the ground? And get all her pretty white curls and fluff dirty? Apparently that crossed a line.

I gave it some more thought while they did some Toss-and-Fetch practice. And had an idea by their next break.

"What about having Little—Bo do a few circles around you before she heads out back along the next spoke? It would be like little circles inside a big circle. Continue the theme." It was unlikely they'd get points for artistic unity, but hey.

"Yeah, that might work."

So she tried to get Little Miss to go in a circle around her. Didn't work. She just didn't seem to understand, and she wasn't too receptive to having Sky lead her around. I realized then how little Little Miss invited physical contact. She wasn't an especially affectionate dog. I don't think I'd ever hugged her.

"Kessie," I called to her as I walked onto the field. Kessie followed eagerly—it's about time!—with her ball in her mouth.

We stood beside Little Miss and Sky. I put out my empty hand. Kessie carefully set her ball into it. "Circle!" I said, and turned around in a circle, her ball visibly in my outstretched hand. She followed it, as I knew she would, making a complete circle around me. "Good dog, good Kessie! What a good dog!" I snuggled her.

"Circle!" I said, and turned again. Kessie again made a circle around me. More praise.

"Circle!" Sky said, getting it immediately, and turned around in a circle, holding the disc out in her hand. Bo walked in a circle around her. "Good Bo, yes!! Good dog!!" She did it again. Bo did it again. "Good Bo! Good!"

I anticipated Sky's next thought. "If you turn a circle too, it makes your next throw more difficult, yes? The dizzy factor?" I'd become a little nauseous.

"Yeah. I could do it though."

"So why not leave the trick as is? With you and Bo both doing the circle inside the circle?" It would be easier on Bo.

So they did their merry-go-round a few more times, adding the inner circle trick after each bring-back.

"Do you think it's still too boring?" Sky asked during their next break.

"You want to add another trick?"

"Yeah. But I don't know what. We have only two more days. But she's good on everything else. She catches almost every throw for the Toss-and-Fetch, and we've got pretty good distance. And she's nailed the Freestyle."

"Which has," I reminded her, "six different throws on your part, alternating high and low catches for Bo, with the inner circle thing after each one—"

"Yeah, but I don't know... It doesn't look nearly as busy as most routines."

"But she's a big dog, and the two of you have had only two weeks. Those people with the busy routines probably have small dogs that tear around like crazy, right? And they've had months to work together on their routines."

"Yeah."

Still, I thought for a moment about something Little Miss could probably add without much practice.

"What about for the last bring-back, instead of dropping it and then doing the circle with you, she sits all pretty and politely gives the disc to you?" She probably had the sit-pretty-and-polite thing already nailed, I thought.

"Okay," she said. Not too excited. I didn't blame her.

But then, in the process of trying to make Little Miss understand she wasn't to drop the disc this one time, Sky discovered quite by accident that she could catch two discs in her mouth at the same time.

"There's your other trick!" I shouted out to Sky before she 'corrected' Little Miss.

"Oh—yeah!" She grinned and did just a little 'woo-hoo' move.

"WE HAVE TO COME up with a final pose," Sky announced the day before the competition. "Most of the guys have their dogs jump into their arms, and they catch them, but I don't think we can make that work."

"Agreed."

"What if she just puts her paws up on me?"

"I don't think Little Miss is allowed to do that," I said. "Her person doesn't really allow her to do any dog things."

She thought about that.

"Maybe Little Miss isn't allowed, but Bo could be. Allowed. Just this once."

I thought about that.

"Yes, I think Bo could be."

So Sky worked on a 'Bo, Up!' command. It didn't take long at all. And I have to say it was a good final pose. With Little— With Bo's paws on Sky's shoulders, and Sky's hands on Bo's waist, they were head to head. Face to face.

COMPETITION DAY ARRIVED. I collected the crew, early, and we went to the field. Grabbed a front row seat.

I almost didn't recognize Sky when she arrived. She had nice white pants on, loose cargo pants or judo pants or something, and a white long-sleeved turtle-neck shirt. And a red bandana. It wasn't until I saw Little Miss run out to greet her that it clicked. Well, actually, it wasn't until Sky put a red bandana around Bo's neck that it clicked. Okay, sometimes I'm slow.

"Hey, cool outfit!"

"Thanks!" She was nervous. Happy-nervous, not scared-nervous.

She put her water bottle and her discs on the ground by all our stuff, then sat on the bleacher. Little Miss tucked herself in front of her. Hm.

"Hey, don't the Freestyle numbers usually have music?" I had a surprise.

"Yeah, but it's optional. And—"

I held out a CD. "Here. It's merry-go-round music. I grabbed it off the internet last night."

She took the CD. "Really?" She looked at it, an odd expression on her face. I was willing to bet no one had ever given her a perfect gift before.

"You have to take it somewhere? To the soundperson or something?"

"Oh. Yeah." She stood up and looked over to where a table and tent had been set up by the organizers.

"And did you already register? Pay the entry fee?"

I saw her eyes suddenly water. She hadn't thought of that. Or hadn't realized.

"'Cuz I'd like to pay," I said smoothly.

"But—"

"Hey, you took care of the work, I'll take care of the money. It's only fair, right?"

She thought about that. "Okay."

She and Bo went to sign in and give the soundperson their

music. And then they returned to wait with us, just looking at all the people, all the dogs, all the excitement.

"You'll do well," I said, "don't worry."

She nodded.

The Toss-and-Fetch went very well. Bo missed just two throws. One, she misjudged, the other was just a bad throw. Hunk didn't care. He howled throughout.

"Well done!" I said to her when she returned to us.

Again, that odd expression on her face. "Thanks," she said. Had no one ever said 'Well done!' to her before? I wanted to reach out and ruffle her hair or something, but it just didn't seem—she was like Little Miss that way.

We watched the other competitors for the next half hour, and then the Freestyle round began. She was fifth up.

"Ladies and Gentlemen, next we have our youngest competitor and a new competitor. Please give a round of applause to Sky and Bo!"

Everyone dutifully applauded, and the two of them walked out to center field. The music began and they started their merry-go-round routine.

I tried to keep Hunk's enthusiasm to a minimum, since I thought it might distract Little Miss. Who was doing very well. Sky improvised a little Harlem-Globetrotter stuff with her discs after some of the inner circles to give Little Miss time to get into position. Nice. As soon as Little Miss caught the last high throw and started to trot back toward the center, Sky casually threw the second disc, which she caught, then, as rehearsed, sat all pretty to give them both to Sky. We started hooting and hollering and howling. They'd nailed it!

And then the final pose. Sky almost lost her balance when Little Miss put her paws up on her shoulders, and then Little Miss almost lost her balance when Sky stepped forward to recover, but they held on to each other and steadied. Body to body, both in white, head to head, both wearing red bandanas, it was perfect.

And then, much to my surprise, Little—Bo gave Sky a kiss. Just a little lick. But still.

Sky's mouth dropped into the broadest smile I'd seen yet. And then she kissed her back.

10

GEESEMASTER

On a hot summer's day, the beginning of a hot summer's week, on my way back from my annual dentist appointment, and so dogless—my dentist charged you if you missed an appointment without cancelling a day ahead, so you dare not be late, but he himself was regularly an hour or more behind schedule—so I'd learned to take a book, and not take the dogs.

Anyway. On a hot summer's day, the beginning of a hot summer's week, on my way back from my annual dentist appointment, when I passed the large and lushly green grounds of some major corporation—I think it was some big publisher, Pearson, or Penguin—something that began with a P—it was their printing and production site—I saw a guy sitting on a park bench watching a bunch of dogs chase a bunch of geese. Behind him was a white van with 'Geesemasters, Inc.' written on the side.

I slowed down—the dogs were having a helluva good time—then decided to pull into the small parking lot before I got rear-ended. The guy turned at the sound of my car and waved.

So I decided to join him on the bench. After the dentist, I could use a few minutes watching dogs having a helluva good time chasing geese.

The man was about fifty, maybe fifty-five, and dressed in what I call 'expensive-casual'. Which is different from 'my casual'.

"Hi," I said. "Mind if I sit?"

"No, not at all. Derek." He extended his hand.

"Brett," I said, shaking it, then sitting down.

"So," I nodded, "the dogs look like they're having an enjoyable time."

"They are. As am I." He sighed with *such* satisfaction. I suspected there was more forthcoming.

"I used to be a CEO. Ainsbury and Associates?"

I shook my head.

"The engineering firm?"

I continued to look clueless. Often not a difficult task, I confess.

"Well, you have no idea what my days were like."

Hang on, just because I don't—he's right. I really have no idea what a CEO does all day. I just know they have lots of power, prestige, and money. And mostly, they don't use it for good.

"And you gave it all up to chase geese?"

He laughed. "The dogs chase the geese. I just sit here. And watch them."

"And you get paid to do that?"

"Well, not what I'm accustomed to, but I do okay. Given."

Given, indeed.

"And the thing of it is," he continued, "when the dogs have chased the geese away from this location? They go over to the pharmaceutical's grounds." He gave a devilish grin. "We have a contract with them as well."

I digested that. "You're telling me you get paid by this company to chase the geese to the other company's grounds, and then you get paid by the other company to chase the geese back to this company's grounds."

"Actually, there's one more company in between that they, and we, go to, but basically, yeah." He chuckled.

"Sweet." Maybe he'd decide that he missed the power, prestige, and money, resume his CEOship, and sell me his Geesemaster business.

Or not. Because he went on, at length, to tell me all about the difference early retirement had made in his life. He'd discovered joy. And peace. And low blood pressure. And he had left this and that and a whole bunch of other things behind.

I nodded, at the appropriate times, I thought—frankly, I was too busy watching the dogs. They were having a *helluva* good time. Zooming in on a bunch of them, sending them all a-flutter to land some distance away, then racing across the grass to their new spot or another bunch of them somewhere else... All except the large one who had left the pack and was now sitting about thirty feet in front of us, in the shade, between two large water dishes, watching the action.

Derek had reached the end of his cv. He didn't ask what I did for a living. Which, of course, was just as well.

"That one's getting on in years?" I nodded to the large dog.

"Yes, that's Whiskey. He was the original Geesemaster, but, yes, he's getting on in years. He has arthritis, but he insists on coming along, being part of the action as best he can."

"Of course," I said, smiling at Whiskey.

"And that one's Pete," he pointed to a small beagle in the distance.

"Pistachio and Truffle," a pair of huskies I couldn't tell apart.

"Greased Lightning," who looked like Spunky Doo on meth.

"And Shazam," a little circus dog mutt.

I watched for another five minutes, then got up to go.

"Well, it's been—"

"Wait—if you would."

I paused. And fanned my damp tshirt to unstick it from my back.

"I have a question. I've been trying to decide whether or not to ask you—" he hesitated, then just went on with it. "I have an opportunity to go to Greece for a week, a couple weeks hence, and I'm looking— I haven't been able to figure out what to do with the dogs. I don't want to leave them at a kennel. Especially Whiskey. None of my friends or acquaintances—you seem like a dog person— Might you possibly be willing to look after them? And take over my contracts for the week?"

Not the question I was expecting.

"I'll pay you, of course," he added.

"Of course," I said.

And then realized he'd been hoping I'd do it for free. Why do people always assume women should just *volunteer* their services?

"Six *is* a lot," I said. But 'Yes!' was what I thought.

"You can stay at my place. Actually, that would be my preference. It would be good to have the house occupied during my absence. And it would be easier on the dogs—"

"I have a couple myself," I said, "we'd have to make sure they're all okay with each other..."

"Have you driven a van before?"

Oh, right. I'd have to use his vehicle as well. His six, plus my two, plus Chum, Hunk, Little Miss, and Spunky Doo—it would be a tight fit even in the dogmobile. God, a dozen dogs. Was I seriously considering this?

Well, I wouldn't have to get the others. What am I saying, of course I would! Have to. Get the others. They'd be expecting me. Every day.

"Why don't you come back to the house—are you free now? You can meet the dogs up close and personal, they can meet you—"

"Okay," I said. I bet he had a swimming pool.

AND A TENNIS COURT, I saw, as I followed him through a gate and up a long driveway. Kessie would—well, no, she'd rather chase tennis balls on grass or sand.

I got out, looked out at all the space—

"It's all fenced in," he said, having already gotten out of his vehicle and let out the dogs. "From as soon as you come through the gate. So—"

"This is all fenced in?"

"Well, with six dogs, a ten by ten pen would hardly do."

Indeed. But this guy had his own dog park. The dogs would love it. I'd bring them all. For the week. It made more sense than picking them up and then dropping them off every day. He hadn't said I couldn't have my friends over.

I followed him inside. Clearly he'd bought the house—the mansion—when he was still a CEO. It wasn't the kind of thing the proprietor of Geesemasters, Inc. could afford.

The dogs each got a snack, and a long drink of water, and then settled themselves in the large living room slash rec room. I joined them. Foregoing the black leather couch for the plushly carpeted floor. Which was where they were. Belly rubs, muscle massages, and ear scratches ensued.

They gave their go-ahead to the plan in a minute. Which was fifty seconds longer than it had taken me to give mine.

Unfortunately, Derek didn't see that. He'd come into the room with a bottle of wine and a couple glasses. Hm. He hadn't asked whether I wanted anything. He hadn't asked what I wanted. He just assumed he knew. What I wanted.

So I waited until he uncorked the bottle and began to pour. "Oh, none for me, thanks, I don't like wine."

"Oh," he said, a little disconcerted.

"I'll take a milkshake though if you have one," I said helpfully.

He just smiled, and sat down. Hm. He hadn't taken me seriously. And I really did want a milkshake.

I looked around, trying to decide what exactly to do. And saw that his wall was covered with albums and CDs, just as Jan's had been covered with books.

He suddenly stood up. I did likewise. Not sure why.

"Sit," he said, "I'm going to play something for you."

What? I looked around for a piano.

He went to one of the walls, pulled out a CD from the shelving, and put it on the stereo. Which wasn't a Pioneer. Or a Kenwood.

Oh. The 'for you' registered. He was performing after all.

"Hear how the conductor draws out the fermata on the fourth note?" He started to give me a play by play, speaking over the best, acoustically speaking, Beethoven I'd ever heard.

"And again, there. That's what I mean by a fermata. It's when a note is made longer than usual. Most conductors rush right by, and the theme loses its gravity. And the contrast in dynamics— And then the crescendo, hear it?"

I didn't react. Please shut up. Oh god, the sound. It surrounded me. Like pure oxygen.

"And there," he tried again, explaining the music to me, "hear how he gives the theme to just the horns?"

My face remained impassive. I was sure of it. Because it took a lot of effort. Oh god, the sound. The *music.*

It was quite clear that he thought my silence indicated that I wasn't understanding what he was saying.

As soon as the movement ended, I stood up again. Reluctantly. Much as I wanted to listen to more, much more, on that exquisite sound system, I couldn't bear to have him ruin it with his incessant chatter.

"So..."

"Oh. Again some time?" he asked.

"I think not."

He looked so surprised. He was, after all, quite a catch, if he did say so himself. Which I'm sure he did. Often.

Would I take the time to explain this? Again? To how many men must I—

"Oh, come on—" he turned on the charm. What he thought was charm. He wasn't going to take 'I think not' for an answer.

All right then.

"When a woman ignores you," I said, "it doesn't necessarily mean she doesn't understand you. Quite likely she does. And is simply, utterly, bored by what you said. Or finds you so patronizing as to be an immediate write-off."

He was stunned.

"Have you ever noticed," I nodded to the stereo as I headed for the door, "how the whole last movement is sort of a tierce de Picardie?" I paused at the door. "A tierce de Picardie is—"

"I know what a tierce de Picardie is," he said irritably.

"Precisely," I said, after a moment. And left.

AND THEN KICKED MYSELF all the way home, thinking I'd blown the chance to have a wonderful week with a dozen dogs at a rich guy's mansion that came with a swimming pool, a wall of CDs, and a sound system to die for.

I CALLED HIM, OF course, to let him know I'd do it. It overlapped with the week I'd agreed to look after Rosie, but I figured I could manage it. Rosie would love the open space. So I called—and left a message. Wasn't sure I'd hear back.

But he didn't have a lot of options.

So a day later, he called back to confirm the arrangement. Left a message.

"...the code for the gate and the back door is double-0-7-double-0-7."

You've got to be kidding.

"That's 0-0-7-0-0-7."

Once more, please? Apparently I'm incapable of maintaining more than two digits in my mind at a time.

"Once more, that's 0-0-7-0-0-7."

I called Chum's person. Sure, he'll love it. And Spunky Doo's person. No problem. Take him. For the whole week. Please. Hunk's person and Little Miss' person were harder sells, but when I mentioned Derek's full name and address, that seemed to do it. Go figure.

WHEN I ARRIVED, I decided to introduce the dogs one at a time to Derek's crew. I let his crew out, waited until they discovered my carful, then opened the front passenger side door to lift out Snookums first. She was, after all, the social butterfly, the diplomat extraordinaire, so I thought she could set the tone—

Not quite what happened. Somehow Spunky Doo scrambled over the back seat—well, probably over Hunk and/or Little Miss—and out the door, followed by Chum and Kessie. And somehow Shazam jumped inside, to say hello to Hunk and Little Miss. Bottom line, though, everyone was cool. There was some concern when Whiskey got knocked over, probably by Spunky Doo—silly me, I'd been mostly concerned about Hunk and the two huskies—but everyone recovered.

I found a folder on the dining room table containing contact info for Derek and his clients, their addresses, and even maps indicating where I should park the vehicle and where I should park myself. I'd intended to just follow the dogs.

THE NEXT DAY, AFTER a very pleasant evening—I'd ordered out for pizza, one for me and several for the dogs—and for a milkshake—Derek had left a bunch of take-out/delivery menus and said I could put the week's food on his account—and then we listened to more Beethoven, and some Bach, and some Chopin...

The next day, after a fun-filled morning, we headed out.

"Time to go to work!" I called out to the dogs. Then laughed.

I had given some thought to the seating arrangement, but basically figured we would do what we were used to, and Derek's crew would go in the back, which is what I assumed they were used to. I hadn't actually paid much attention when he'd loaded them up, and they were already out when I'd pulled up behind him at his house.

So I opened the driver's door of the van and lifted Kessie in. Then I walked around to open the front passenger side door. Chum jumped in, and I lifted Snookums in after him.

Then I opened the back passenger door. Whiskey stepped up. Okay, that's where he went. He waited at the open door, looking eagerly at the back seat. Ah. Right. He needed a boost. I gave him one. Hunk and Little Miss joined him from the other side. Okay, good, Whiskey had no problem with that.

Then I opened the back door, and sure enough, the rest of Derek's crew jumped in. Pistachio, Truffle, Greased Lightning, Shazam, and with a little help, Pete. Spunky Doo joined them. Good.

No wait. Not good. I reached in for Pete and Shazam. They'd get trampled. So I carried them up to the front seat, and asked Chum to get in the back. Easy-going Chum, he was okay with that. Thanks.

I got in the driver's seat, Kessie settling on my lap, then counted: one, two, three, four, five, six, seven, eight, nine, ten, eleven—I'm missing one. Oh, Shazam had jumped into the back seat. Okay. I turned the ignition. Shazam jumped back into the front seat. Somersaulted into the front seat, actually. Perhaps he really *had* been a circus dog.

I drove around and out the convenient circular driveway, through the gate, then turned left onto the road.

It became immediately apparent that Spunky Doo was a bowling ball.

"Spunky Doo!" I called out to him as I saw, in the rear-view mirror, two of the other four dogs go down with him. He popped up and looked at me. "Careful!" I said.

Another turn, three dogs down. "Spunky Doo!" He popped up and looked at me again. And grinned. And then I knew he was doing it on purpose.

I DROVE TO MONDAY'S location. I had met Derek and his crew at Friday's location, so this was a different one. I had no trouble finding the place, surprisingly enough, or the parking lot. Free at last, free at last, thank god we're free at last! Yeah, yeah.

All of the dogs took off up the hill, except for Kessie who insisted I throw her ball for her, so she could chase it up the hill. I hauled out the water dishes and jugs, and walked after them. It was a pleasant sunny summer's day.

As soon as I crested the hill—shit.

Snookums had caught a goose.

And everyone had frozen.

I yelled at her. Okay, screamed is more like it.

Kessie took advantage of the stoppage of time to slip her bright green tennis ball into my hand.

Derek's crew, with the exception of Whiskey, was probably thinking, We can *do* that? We're allowed? I suspect Whiskey was thinking, Hot damn, she's good!

As for my crew, Chum, Hunk, and Little Miss— Spunky Doo hadn't noticed that time had stopped. He was off doing—please tell me he's not rolling in goose shit. Shit. As for Chum, Hunk, and Little Miss, they seemed to be having trouble deciding whether what Snookums had done was against the rules. Geese weren't exactly wild. But nor were they clearly pets. I suspect Hunk finally cast the deciding vote: you don't kill someone else's toys.

As for me, I was thinking, Why the *hell* hadn't I anticipated this?

Well, because the geese were bigger than her. Not by much, agreed. She wasn't quite the six pound puppy she once was. But still.

And geese can fly, right? So how the hell had she *caught* a goose?

And don't they poke at you when they're angry? So how the *hell* had she *caught* a goose?

Still. She had.

I unfroze and broke into a trot. Please be dead, please be dead, don't make me finish the job—Snookums gave the bird a good shake.

For the record, a medium-sized goose is far more amenable to shaking than a flying disc.

She shook it again. The head flew off. Okay, so that meant it had to be dead, right? Or can geese, like chickens, run around with their heads chopped off?

Speaking of geese running around, the flock had fled. No surprise there.

When I got to the scene of the crime, all the dogs looked at me. Now what?

“Well,” I said, “our job here is done.” I turned to go.

What?

“Back to the van,” I said, to a dozen—eleven disappointed dog faces. “We’re here to chase geese. There are no more geese here. Ergo, we’re done.”

Halfway back to the van, I stopped. What about the dead goose? I can’t just leave it there.

Well, why not? Something will probably come in the middle of the night and carry it off, right?

Yeah, but what if ‘something’ doesn’t? When we come back, a few days hence, it’ll be a rotting mess crawling with maggots. I thought of Spunky Doo. And got side-tracked wondering whether the Kleenex in my pocket would do. For today.

Back on topic, I realized I had to bury the goose.

But I had nothing to bury it with.

Could I toss it into the decorative pond?

It would probably surface, all bloated and—I thought of Spunky Doo.

I had to take it with me. I could bury it back home. At Derek’s place. Yes. In the farthest corner.

I returned to the goose. The dogs followed.

No, I needed a plastic bag, at least. I headed back to the van. The dogs were, understandably, annoyed. Are we coming or going?

No plastic bag. No empty cardboard box. No nothing.

I returned to the goose, folded the bloody parts into the good parts as best I could and picked it up.

Snookums was overjoyed. We’re taking it home? *We’re taking it home!!*

I couldn't put it in the back. Or in the back seat. Okay, the front passenger footwell. I'd drive slowly so no one would fall down onto—into—the goose.

Okay, done.

"Give," I said to Snookums, who had been all the while happily at my side, supervising. I reached down to take the neck—wait a minute, where's the head? Where did the head go?

Don't worry about it, I told myself, surely the vultures or buzzards or whatever will take care of it.

I lifted Snookums into the front seat—she wouldn't let go of the neck, of course—what had I been thinking—then Pete and Shazam. Kessie into the driver's seat. Whiskey, then Hunk and Little Miss into the back seat. The rest—one, two, three, four, five.

Okay, good to go.

Two turns later, I heard someone throwing up in the back. I glanced in the rear-view mirror to see Spunky Doo heaving mightily. Okay, now I know where the head had gone.

THROUGH THE GATE, UP the driveway, into the circle. I let the dogs out, then put them all inside. Found a shovel in the garage, buried the goose at the far edge of the property, just inside the fence. Went inside, made a margarita, put on some Brian Eno.

LATER, JUST BEFORE DARK and we were all inside, I realized we weren't all inside. Snookums was missing. I'd forgotten to close the doggy door. Shit.

I found a flashlight and went outside. Straight to the freshly dug grave. Now freshly undug.

"Snookums!"

What? She looked at me, standing in the middle of the remains of a pillow fight. A somewhat bloody pillow fight.

WHERE WAS A DUMPSTER when you needed one, I was asking myself half an hour later, as I cruised up and down the streets, a body neatly bundled up in a hefty bag sitting in the back.

Aha! I pulled up beside the dumpster, got out, opened the back door, lifted out my bundle, then—

"Freeze!"

What?

"Don't move! Stay where you are!"

Remain immobile, yeah, I get that, but—why?

"That dumpster belongs to ABC Industries," the security guard said, "and it's illegal to dump—what is that?"

He looked suspiciously at my bundle.

"Oh, god," he cried, "are you doing what I think you're doing?"

He spoke quickly and urgently into his walkie-talkie. "I have a 629 in progress. 2867 Progress Boulevard, freight entrance. That's a 629 in progress at 2867 Progress Boulevard, freight entrance."

"What's a 629?" I asked. Innocently enough.

"Put the—package—down, M'am. I don't know what your circumstances are, and I know you must have felt very desperate to have done what you have done, but all of God's children—"

What? I was suddenly feeling very much like Spunky Doo. I had definitely missed a memo. Or two.

"You can't just dump your baby in a dumpster, Ma'm."

"What? This isn't a baby! It's a goose. An adult goose." I bent down to unwrap the body.

"Stop!" He pointed his laser gun at me. "Do not tamper with the evidence."

"What evidence? My dog killed a goose. I buried it, but she dug it up. Garbage pick-up where I'm staying isn't for another week. So I just thought—"

The sirens drowned out the rest of my explanation.

THE POLICE WHO ARRIVED, at the freight entrance of ABC Industries, 2867 Progress Boulevard, had the same attitude toward tampering with the evidence, so an hour later, I found myself in a cell. I'd been charged and processed. Inexplicably, no one had yet opened the package.

An hour after that, I realized, given the way things were going, it was possible that I'd spend the night there. The dogs! I had to call someone to go look after the dogs. They'd—mine, at least—Snookums and Kessie, at least—would be worried if I didn't come home. I'd left the doggy door open, I think, so they could go out if they needed to, and several would have needed to by now, but—oh god, what if Snookums decided to go after a raccoon next?

Jocko's person and Carson's person, they both had jobs—Jan? No, it'd be too much. With Biscuit and Cookie, that'd make fourteen—Winner's person, I hardly knew her. Not Meredith either. Amber's person was probably away on an SAR. Sky—is a thirteen-or-fourteen-year-old old enough to be allowed to stay overnight by herself? I thought Sky would be fine, actually. She was a smart, responsible young woman. But how would she get to Derek's house? It wasn't exactly near a bus route. It was night—driving her bike there was probably not a good idea. And I doubted that either of her parents would drive her. Okay, what about Charmaine? Shit! This was Monday! I was supposed to pick up Rosie tonight—Charmaine was leaving tomorrow morning for the trials. Okay, this really complicated things.

No, I thought a minute later, it might actually simplify things. I called Charmaine and explained the situation. Could she drive Rosie to Derek's house, picking up Sky on the way? Then get Sky settled, make sure she's okay?

She was a little bit nervous about leaving Rosie not only at a strange place, but also with a strange person, but there was no way around it.

"I could be back later tonight yet," I said. "Don't even *think* about missing the trials. She'll be fine. The whole place is fenced in. The other dogs are good. Sky's good, you'll see."

"Okay," she agreed, reluctantly.

"Leave your phone number with Sky, and I'll call you as soon as I get there," I said. I didn't want her to be distracted from her race with worry about Rosie.

So then I crossed my fingers and called Sky.

"Hey, Sky, it's Brett, how are you?"

"Okay..."

"Listen, I'm in a bit of a—are you free tonight?"

There was the slightest of pauses. "Let me check my social calendar. Nope, tonight is the cotillion."

Okay, she'd developed sarcasm since I last saw her. Cool.

I told her my situation. Oddly enough, or not, my being in jail didn't faze her. And she agreed immediately to look after the dogs.

"Don't you have to ask your parents first?"

"No," she said after the briefest of moments. "I'll leave a note," she added cryptically.

I gave her Charmaine's phone number so she could call to confirm our arrangement and tell Charmaine where she lived.

"Okay," I said, "so there's my two, you remember Kessie and Snookums, and the other four are there too, Hunk, Chum, Spunky Doo, and Little—Bo. And there will be Rosie, Charmaine's dog, a greyhound.

"The other guy's dogs, you should probably know their names," I said. "Pete's the little beagle, he's teaching Snookums how to howl. The other little one is Shazam. Then there's Pistachio and Truffle, they're twins, I think, huskies. Greased Lightning, you'll know which one that is. And the big one, that's Whiskey. He's old, so you might have to help him with the stairs. And if doesn't seem to be paying attention to him, it's just that his hearing is going."

"I'll talk loud to him, or make sure he sees me," she said.

"Good. Okay, they'll all be safe enough, the yard is fenced in, you just need to give them food, water, snuggles—oh, and be sure to close the doggy door once they're all in. That's important."

I gave her the address and the 'double 07 double 07' code for the gate and the door.

"Seriously?" she said. "Double 07? Twice?"

What I thought!

"Before you leave your house, look up the phone number for Dr. Vail. V-A-I-L. She's a vet. Take it with you. If you have any problem with the dogs, call Dr. Vail. Tell her I'll pay for a house call."

"Okay, got it."

I made her repeat the address and I reminded her again about the doggy door. I also told her to tell Charmaine to make sure the gate closed behind her when she left, and then the guard said I had to hang up.

NEXT MORNING, I WAS released—all charges were dropped once someone finally opened the package. I pulled in through the gate, up to the house, and saw Sky at the side playing Frisbee with Little Miss. And, it looked like, Pistachio and Truffle. Cool.

Kessie came running to me from a spot in the shady spectator's area. You're home! You're home! She put her tennis ball into my hand.

Snookums also came running to me, howling. Sort of. Woo-grg. Woo-grg. She grinned at me. I think. Hard to tell with a goose feather in her mouth.

I looked at Sky with raised eyebrows.

"I said she could have it. She isn't chewing it or anything. I don't think she's going to try to swallow it."

"Okay, good, but where—"

"First thing this morning, I found, well, she led me straight to it. Where you buried the goose. She was digging there again. So I thought if I let her, if she could dig until she was convinced the goose wasn't there anymore, then she wouldn't keep going back to dig."

"Ah."

"When she was done, I filled it in. Put the grass back over top. Then I gave her a bath."

I raised my eyebrows again.

"She really needed one and I didn't think the rich guy would appreciate—"

"Good call." I looked around then for the others.

"I put Spunky Doo inside," Sky said, casually tossing another disc for the dogs, "and closed the door."

"Good thinking."

"Whiskey's there, in the shade," she pointed, and I saw that Hunk was with him. Spectating Little Miss.

"Chum's in the swimming pool doing laps," she continued to take inventory. "I double-checked that he could get out okay." And he could indeed, as he proved then by coming to say hi with a welcome shower.

"And—" I looked around. There were still a few unaccounted for.

"Rosie and Greased Lightning are racing."

At that very moment, they zoomed by us in a blur. I broke into a smile. I hadn't anticipated that. But of course! Greased Lightning had possibly not met his match until Rosie. And Rosie—

"Charmaine told me what happened to Rosie," she added. "That's awful."

"Yes," I agreed. What more could be said?

"But she's happy now."

"Indeed she is," I said as the two of them zoomed by again. "This may be the first time she's raced with another dog since what happened to her," I said.

"Really?" Sky smiled then. "Once I realized that's what they wanted to do, I checked for holes. I didn't want either of them to break a leg," she explained. "But the guy who lives here, he must have a groundskeeper or something because it's pretty good. There was one spot, though. I filled it in."

"And—" I looked around. Still a few unaccounted for—

"And Pete and Shazam are inside with Spunky Doo," Sky finished her report.

"Excellent!" I said to her. I was truly impressed. "Good job!!"

She beamed.

"So," I said, looking at my watch, "I guess I should drive you to school."

"It's lunch," she said. Without enthusiasm. "And then there's just two classes—couldn't I—"

"Stay for dinner?" I understood. Immediately. "We're having pizza," I added. As if that really mattered.

She couldn't contain her smile.

I insisted she call her parents though, but I suspected it wasn't really necessary. It had not gone unnoticed by me that neither her mother nor her father had come to see her at the competition. Her brother hadn't even bothered to cheer her on, and he was there.

I thought about asking her about her home life, but then realized this was a holiday for her. *From* her home life.

AT AROUND NINE O'CLOCK, I got ready to take her back. The dogs weren't expecting to go anywhere since it was night, which made things easier, and besides, they were all tuckered out from their day despite it having been a non-geesemaster day. They had been disc dogging, swimming, racing, chasing tennis balls, and just generally romping around with each other...

Sky desultorily packed up her stuff. Rolled up the sleeping back she'd brought, put her stuff back into her knapsack.

I'd written out a cheque. "Here," I said, "for services rendered."

She took it, confused, saw the amount, and her eyes widened.

"But—"

"Fifteen hours, right?" I asked. "You got here around eight, I didn't get back until around eleven."

"Yeah, but—when I babysit—"

"Your brother, he cuts grass or something?"

"Yeah."

"How much does he get? An hour."

"Twenty, I think."

"Well, dogs are way more important than grass. And you had thirteen of them to look after."

"Yeah, but I was sleeping for—"

"You were still on duty. If something had happened in the middle of the night, you would have had to be responsible. Take it, Sky. You earned it. Don't think you didn't."

She tucked it into her knapsack, then slung it over her shoulder.

"Oh wait," she unslung it and dug out her discs. "You should have one."

I agreed. Part of our afternoon had been spent with flying disc lessons. I'd failed. Miserably. And so needed to practice. Despite the fact that another part of our afternoon had been spent making covert arrangements for Sky to play with Bo in the field two or three times a week. I regretted not having thought of that sooner.

"What color do you want?"

I took a look. "I'll take the pink one."

"Seriously? You are *so* not pink."

"Why thank you!"

Wednesday was another geesemaster day. And another seating arrangement challenge. Adding Rosie, the bunch in the back didn't fit. In the back.

The front seat was full. The back seat was full. I considered leaving Whiskey at home, but that would break his heart.

I considered putting Chum in the front passenger seat footwell, but he wouldn't fit. Pete and Shazam fit, so I considered putting Chum into the front passenger seat as usual, but what if Chum or Snookums fell down onto Pete or Shazam, which was likely since they were sharing the front seat. Only Kessie fit on my lap.

I tried having Hunk and Little Miss move over, but there really was no 'over' to move to.

If the vehicle had a bench seat, like mine—aha! I went into the garage, looking for a board or—a cardboard box! And a lounge chair cushion!

I mangled the cardboard box into place and put the cushion on top, turning the front bucket seats into a bench seat. Kessie on my lap, Chum at the other end, Snookums, Pete, and Shazam in between. Back seat as it was. Back as it was, Rosie replacing Chum.

Good to go.

But all for nothing. There were no geese at the designated second location. Did I come to the wrong place? Had I gotten my days mixed up? No.

Maybe the geese had. Maybe they had gone to the wrong place or gotten their days mixed up.

So I drove to the third location, Friday's location. No geese.

Just for the hell of it, I drove to the first location. Where it all began... No geese there either. Perhaps they were suffering from PTSD and had left the city. Maybe even the country.

For a while, we just drove around, looking for the geese. The phrase 'a wild goose chase' came to mind. Except for the fact that *there were no geese to chase*! I glared at Snookums.

Eventually, we went home. There was nothing more we could do.

SO INSTEAD OF CHASING geese, we had a leisurely afternoon in the summer sun watching butterflies and— Well, actually, there weren't any butterflies—have they all gone extinct already? I couldn't remember the last time I saw a butterfly, I realized with horror.

I made a margarita and settled into a very comfortable chair by the pool. Kessie set her ball oh-so-carefully into my oh-so-casually dangling hand. I threw it into the pool. It's a hot day! Go for a swim, Kessie! She ran to the edge of the pool, then watched it plop into the water. She stared at it for a moment, then barked at it, willing it to bob closer and closer to her. But it wouldn't. After a few seconds, she gave up and ran inside. A minute later, she ran back outside, to me, another ball in her mouth. Which she set oh-so-carefully into my oh-so-casually dangling hand...

Whiskey lay in the shade nearby, Rosie and Greased Lightning ran a couple laps, Chum swam a couple laps (Kessie's ball in his mouth), Shazam did some cute tricks off the diving board, Spunky Doo did some spectacular tricks off the diving board, Pete continued to teach Snookums how to howl, Hunk and Little Miss went for a stroll around the grounds, Pistachio and Truffle chewed away on their chew toys—and then the phone rang.

I stared at it. It hadn't rung all week. One of Derek's clients calling to fire us—him? Having seen us *not* there? Derek just checking in?

I answered it.

"Hello?"

"Hello, is this Geesemasters?"

"Yes? I mean, Yes, how can I help you?"

"We'd like to hire you."

"What?"

"A bunch of geese showed up at our grounds early in the week and, well, they're making quite a mess. City ordinance prevents us from shooting them or poisoning them, so—"

"Yes! I mean, yes, we can help you out with that, sir. Mr. Ainsbury is out of the country at the moment, but I'd be glad to bring the crew over later today, and you can sort out the paper work with him when he returns next week. Will that be sufficient?"

"Yes, that'd be great." He gave me the address and directions.

AN HOUR LATER WE were there.

I'd thoughtfully put Snookums' harness on her, carefully putting it over the feather in her mouth—she'd taken to taking it everywhere—clipped the harness to her leash, and tied her leash to the emergency brake. So when I opened the door—Free at last! Free at last! Thank—Thank god she wasn't able to get out and kill another goose.

Thank god, too, the others had forgotten what she'd done and/or had not treated it as a lesson in How to Spruce up Your Job

Performance.

Because when I followed the dogs to the geese in the distance, I could see that things were back to normal. With two exceptions—Kessie on my left, her ball in her mouth, Snookums on my right, leashed—everyone was simply having a helluva good time chasing the geese.

Were they our geese? I had no way of telling. And it didn't really matter. No one had called to fire Derek *and* I'd gotten him an additional client. Was I ready for that promotion or what?

We continued to walk toward the geese, stopping every now and then so I could accept Kessie's ball and throw it for her. When we got close enough for Snookums to see them, she stopped, looked at me, and cringed. Notwithstanding the feather in her mouth, the last time a goose, her, and me were in the same picture, I'd yelled at her. Time before that when a goose, her, and me were in the same picture, I'd yelled at her.

"It's okay, sweetheart," I assured her, and bent down snuggle her. "I understand. And you're still my little Snookums, my little Geesemaster."

She squiggled in delight. Yes, she was. My little Snookums. *The* Geesemaster.

11

NISHA

About a month later, we had Rosie again. Charmaine had made the national team and was away at her first international meet. They were grooming her for big things. Very big things.

So basically we went to the beach every day instead of alternating dog park, beach, field, and whatever. There had been lots of whatever lately, so every day at the beach sounded good to me.

Typically we had the beach to ourselves. Rosie would take off to sprint up and down, nudging her nose into my hip each time she returned before taking off again, literally touching base. Chum and Hunk typically took to the water, the latter vocalizing so uncharacteristically, Snookums usually trotted along the edge, splish splash, plunk plunk, Kessie chased her ball, Little Miss caught her pink flying disc, and Spunky Doo did whatever the hell he wanted.

But today, we were earlier than usual—it was almost still morning—and someone else was there. A woman, just standing there, not walking, with a black lab—on a leash. At the beach! Seriously?

We—all but Rosie, who had already taken off—headed toward them to say hi, Snookums leading the way.

Hurry! she said to me, running ahead, then running back, then running ahead, then running back, stretching the now-you-see-it-now-you-don't umbilical cord between us.

Once I was close enough, she just ran right up to the dog. It turned and snapped at her.

Surprised, but with great reflexes, Snookums did an about-face and flew into my arms. She hadn't done that since about five pounds ago, so she didn't quite make it, and I stumbled to catch her as she tumbled down my legs.

"I'm so sorry," the woman said, pulling the dog awkwardly closer to her.

I picked Snookums up and made sure Kessie was behind me. Hunk and Little Miss had stepped up, Chum as well, and Spunky Doo—god knows where Spunky Doo was.

"Nisha's really quite nice," the woman continued to apologize, "it's just that—"

Chum had given me his beach ball, then stepped forward to be nose to nose with Nisha. Who was quivering, clearly anxious.

"—she's blind."

Oh. Oh.

"No, I'm sorry," I said. "I shouldn't've let Snookums—"

Chum was making everything right. He was sort of nuzzling Nisha, then sort of stroking her with his head. She was calming. She was even wagging her tail a little.

"Shall we walk?" I said, nodding up the beach. Rosie flew toward us, nudged my hip, then took off again. Spunky doo chased after her. Like a Jalopy after a Porsche.

"Sure," she replied. "This way," she said to Nisha and gently turned her. Chum positioned himself at her side. They were actually touching. Mirror images, I thought, they were such a close match except for color.

"I'm Brett," I said, then asked, curious, "So, what happened?" She couldn't have been blind from birth if she was having so much trouble.

"Anju," we shook hands. A little awkwardly since Snookums was still in my arms. I would've set her down, but she was having none of that.

"Well," Anju said, "I went to work one day and when I came home, Nisha was blind."

I must have looked shocked.

"They call it SARDS. Sudden Acquired Retinal Degeneration Syndrome. They know it tends to happen with middle-aged dogs who have been spayed, but they don't know why. Apparently there's no pain, but—"

"No physical pain, maybe—"

"Yes!" She looked at me in surprise. I got it.

I'd noticed Chum was staying by Nisha's side.

"Do you think you could let Nisha off the leash? She seems comfortable walking beside Chum."

"I don't know," she stopped and looked out at the beach. "I do let her off the leash in our yard—it's all fenced in. But—" she resumed walking, keeping Nisha leashed. "At first it was like she didn't know she was blind. She woke up one day and didn't see the tree in the back, so it didn't exist."

"So she ran right into it." I set Snookums down, took Kessie's ball and threw it ahead of us, then threw Little Miss' disc behind us. Then picked up Snookums again.

She nodded.

"Then when she figured it out, she just got so afraid."

"Understandably so." I thought of Jocko, never knowing when some monster was going to come out of nowhere and hurt him.

"She seems content on the leash, but—she loves—she used to love—"

Anju took a moment.

"This—coming here—this was her heaven. I'd let her off, she'd run around a bit, then she'd hit the water and swim forever.

"And I didn't want her to lose that too, so—first we tried with her still leashed. I brought an extra long rope. But she kept getting tangled in it.

"So then I thought, what if I got a dinghy or something and paddled alongside her."

"Did that work?"

"No, between her swimming into it and me hitting her with the paddle—

"So then I thought I'll just walk along in the shallow water and constantly talk to her, call out to her, so she can use stay oriented—"

"That sounds reasonable," I interjected.

"Yes, but—"

The woman was near tears.

"—she started veering out, so I call her back, but she must've gotten water in her ears or something because she turned out instead of in, and I kept calling, but she couldn't hear me."

Of course. I thought of how dogs out in the country prefer to walk on the 'wrong' side of the road, facing oncoming cars, with their ears, the better to hear them coming.

"Then she got totally disoriented, and she must have panicked—she started to swim really hard, first in circles, then straight out.

"I went after her, but I don't swim— I kept calling, but she was completely beside herself. I was afraid she was going to drown."

Anju paused for a moment. I threw Kessie's ball and Little Miss' disc again.

"I went as far as I could, up to my chin— screaming her name, sobbing, actually, she went under once, exhausted and in terror, and I thought I was going to see her die right before my eyes—"

My god, it must have been awful. For both of them. I imagined swimming here, in the ocean—well, it's not really the ocean, but it may as well be—blind. No landmarks whatsoever, nothing to tell you right, left, forward, backward—you couldn't just pick a direction then go straight, should that be possible, until you hit the edge of the pool.

Then I imagined seeing Kessie or Snookums, or any of them, drowning right in front of me.

"She started swimming in circles again, and I screamed her name every time she faced me—she must have finally heard me, because she turned in again, and when she got close enough, I lunged and grabbed her, before she turned again and headed out—but then I lost my feet and I went under—"

"But you saved her—she's here," I stated the obvious.

"Yes, but now when we come, she usually—she refuses to move. It's like she's paralyzed in one spot. I have to coax her to even walk. I ruined the one thing she had left," she was in tears now, absolutely miserable with guilt. "The one thing she loved most of all."

"She's walking now," I said.

"She is," Anju agreed, wiping her face.

"And," I nodded to Chum and Nisha, "they seem to be gluing themselves to each other. Why don't you try letting her off the leash? She can use him as a reference point, look, she sort of keeps nudging him, or he keeps nudging her—"

She watched them carefully and saw that it was so.

"And I can swim," I added.

"Okay," she agreed to try it. "Nisha," she bent to unclip her leash, "I'm going to unclip you." Nisha just stood there for a second, frozen, but then Chum stepped even closer to her, and they resumed walking.

"So how has she been at home?" I set Snookums down again— she was heavy!— threw ball and disc, and we continued walking as well. Snookums agreed to follow on her own. Beside Hunk.

"Home's not so much a problem. Inside, I've left everything pretty much the way it was. And we've lived there forever, so she has a good mental map. I just make sure I leave everything in the same spot."

"Her mental map is probably reinforced with scent," I said. "You know, the kitchen probably smells, well, like the kitchen, and if you always keep your shoes at the back door—"

"You're probably right," she said. "I hadn't thought of that. I did quickly discover that I needed to pad all the sharp edges at her height. Got rid of the coffee table in the living room altogether. And I put a gate across the top of the stairs to the basement.

"There are stairs at the back door out to the yard—it's a porch, not a patio—and we're counting them—one, two, three, *four*—so she knows when she's at the bottom. I'm thinking of putting a ramp there instead, but I don't know whether that would be more confusing."

"And the yard's fenced in?"

"Yes, so it's safe enough, but I spent a week planting a hedge along the inside perimeter. It hurts less to run into a hedge than a wooden fence," she explained. "But still, she gets lost sometimes. I have to watch."

"What if you gave her a scent map of the yard?"

She looked at me curiously.

"Like if you planted, I don't know, mint along the back hedge, but something different along the sides. Roses—no they have thorns—some other flower, maybe—along the sides. Maybe she'd figure out as long as she follows the daisies away from the mint, or whatever, she'll get back to the porch."

Anju thought about that.

"That wouldn't work in winter though—"

Hm. "Maybe you could get some sort of spray—no, that would probably kill the hedges."

"Maybe there's something that wouldn't kill them. Whenever I'm out cleaning up after her, which I do almost every day now anyway, she stepped in her own mess once, poor thing—"

"Hey! You could just dump her messes into the side bushes! So all she need do is follow *that* smell away from the mint, to get back to the house!"

I saw that Chum had gradually gone into the water. Nisha had followed. Close. They were splish splashing side by side. Anju, ever vigilant, had noticed as well. She looked at me eagerly and smiled.

"And I vocalize a lot," she continued then. "I talk to her all day now, just letting her know where I am, what I'm doing. It's weird, not that I would have wanted this, but we're much closer now that she's blind. She depends on me for everything. And so I have to pay such close attention to her. She trusts me to let her know, when we're out walking for instance, when there's a curb. I've taught her up and down."

"You're her seeing eye person!"

Anju laughed. "Yes!"

"It's sad though," she said a minute later, "not to make eye contact with her. I miss that the most. When she looks at me now, there's such a vacant—"

"She can still play tug of war with you though, she can still chew on her chew toys."

"That's the thing," she said. "She was never really into any of that. Swimming. That was it. That was all. That was everything for her," she added, sadly.

Rosie came running back then, and touched base, nudging her nose to my hip. Spunky Doo followed, and knocked me over.

Snookums licked my face.

Kessie set her ball into my hand.

Little Miss dropped her disc onto my stomach.

Anju extended her hand and helped me back up.

And then we saw that Chum and Nisha had gone even further into the water. In fact, they were swimming!

"Look!" I said to Anju. "She's swimming. Nisha's swimming!"

Anju turned and—Nisha was indeed swimming. She was just barely in water over her head. But she was. And she was swimming, close beside Chum. Maybe she smelled him, or heard his breathing, or felt the water churning slightly—whatever, they were swimming side by side, less than a foot from each other.

Anju looked at me in joy.

"Let's keep walking," I said. "And talking."

"Good girl, I'm here," Anju called out. That seemed to give her additional confidence—Nisha swam harder.

So we continued to walk, and talk, and Anju continued to call out to Nisha. Every thirty seconds. Which seems excessive, but, as I had imagined, even half a minute without any bearings is a long time.

"ICE CREAM?" WE HAD reached the turnaround spot.

"Yes! It's her second-favorite thing about being here!" she laughed.

"Chum!" I called out.

"Nisha! Come in!" she waded into the water, to be better heard. "This way!"

Nisha turned toward Anju's voice, but then for some reason changed her mind and turned the wrong way. Hm. Maybe calm open water does something to the directionality of sound. I wondered if it had been calm the day of their trauma. Surely if it had been windy, I thought, Nisha would have realized she was swimming out, *into* the waves.

"This way, Nisha! This way!" Anju started to panic, and I quickly went to stand beside her in the water, ready to—

But Chum had been paying attention. He swam not just *to* Nisha, but *into* her, nudging her, corralling her, toward shore.

"Nicely done!" I told him. Winn and sheep herding dogs worldwide would have been proud.

MINT FOR KESSIE, BUTTER Pecan for Snookums, Tiger Tail Licorice for Hunk, French Vanilla for Little Miss. Rosie? I asked for a taster of Coconut Pie. Yes. And Spunky Doo—No, no Espresso Express today, how about Bubblegum? Okay.

Spunky Doo jumped in the air. I'm getting bubblegum! he told everyone.

"No. Not bubblegum," I said firmly. "Bubblegum *ice cream.*"

God forbid.

Peanut Butter Swirl for Chum and— "What does Nisha like?" I asked Anju.

"Birthday Cake," she said.

Especially appropriate today, I thought.

Triple Chocolate Brownie Fudge for me. Anju had Strawberry and Cream.

We all settled in the sand, everyone giving Nisha some space, seeming to understand that something was not quite right. Except, of course, for Spunky Doo, for whom 'not quite right' was the norm, and Chum, who lay full-length beside her, so she was sandwiched between him and Anju.

"And there's no cure?" I asked, failing to convince Snookums that she did not need to be in my lap.

"There is," Anju said. "And the sooner you get the treatment, the better. They say within two months."

I looked at her.

"We're scheduled for Thursday. But they warn you that even after the treatment, your dog won't be catching frisbees," she smiled at Little Miss. "They'll improve enough to get around, but—"

"But here," I looked out at the wide open beach, the open expanse of water, "she'll still be, for all intents and purposes, blind."

Anju nodded.

"Hey," I said a moment later, "you should bring a flashlight. A big, bright one. You could be a mobile lighthouse for her."

"That's a good idea," she said thoughtfully, making a mental note.

And then we talked about other stuff. Women's experience of group behavior, for example. Anju was a Sociology prof at the university.

"My colleagues—and I use that word loosely," she said, "keep trying to push my work off to the side, saying I'm investigating special case phenomena."

"But women's experience isn't special case, it's a full half of human experience," I said.

"Yes! And it is typically different from the other half!"

"Which is," I said, "typically presented as representative of the whole."

"Yes!"

AFTER A WHILE, WE headed back. Chum and Nisha chose to swim again. And we both saw how subtly he kept her straight, how he always kept himself between her and the open water, keeping her between him and Anju.

ONCE BACK AT THE car, I gave Anju Chum's phone number. I told her that I was sure his people would be delighted if she wanted to pick him up every day and take him to the beach to swim with Nisha.

"Really?" She couldn't believe it. "Every day?"

"I wouldn't be surprised," I said. "He comes to our place every day, in the afternoon, to join us for our walk or whatever. You could pick him up every day, in the morning, to join you for your swim."

And so it was that Chum became Nisha's safe swimming buddy. And Nisha was able to resume doing the one thing she loved most of all.

12

THE TWELVE DAYS AT SPOILED SILLY

It was early September. And a beautiful day. I had planned a field trip, since it had been a while, but then I got a call from the temp agency. I had a job interview, last minute, later that afternoon. So the dog park it was.

AS SOON AS I let the four of them out—I didn't have time to get Hunk and Little Miss—we heard it. It sounded like someone was playing the accordion and a little dog was singing along. Sure enough, that's exactly what it was. At the near end of the first romping area, a woman was sitting on a chair, playing an accordion. A little dog was sitting in her lap, singing along.

Snookums looked at me for permission, and I nodded. She ran toward them, then stopped a few feet short. She politely sat down, an audience. Then she started howling along. Wooooo wooooo. She looked back at me, proudly. Wooooo wooooo woooo. Note to self, get an accordion.

Chum and Kessie weren't into howling, but Spunky Doo surprised me by going to sit beside Snookums and joining in. He was joyously out of tune.

There was no open accordion case for coins, so I assumed the woman was there just because it was a pleasant place to be, playing her accordion for her dog in the middle of a grassy field. Or perhaps her neighbors had insisted.

We lingered for a few minutes, then carried on through the park taking our shortest route. I glanced at my watch occasionally.

At the exit, or entrance, depending on whether you're coming or going, truly a problem for Spunky Doo most of the time, there was a bulletin board. It had the Dog Park Rules in the center, which everyone read, and most people respected, and the rest of the space was plastered with the usual notices: lost dogs, puppies free to a good home, puppies for sale (didn't matter what kind of home), obedience classes, and so on.

Today, there was a new notice. An advertisement for a place called Spoiled Silly: a combination spa, salon, and studio. Interesting concept, I thought. They were offering an opening discount for two whole weeks. As of two days ago. Cool. I tore off one of the address and phone number tabs and tucked it in my pocket.

I DROPPED OFF SPUNKY Doo, then went home. Chum, as usual, said thank you and trotted on home. I showered, put on some clean clothes, told Kessie and Snookums I'd be back soon, then drove to City Hall.

I found Human Resources, and joined six other waiting women. Not a surprise—it was a temp clerical job. (What other kind was there for women?) All six were costumed in femininity.

Half an hour later, I was ushered into the interview room and introduced to a Mr. Peppler. One of the first questions Mr. Peppler asked was why hadn't I dressed up a bit. I suspected the question wasn't on his list.

"You mean, why didn't I wear a skirt or a dress?"

He nodded.

"What, you want to see my legs?" I asked.

"N-no," he stammered.

"Then why did you want me to wear a skirt or a dress?"

He couldn't say.

For a second, I considered rolling up my pants, but I thought he'd probably faint when he saw that I had actual hair on my legs.

"Is it relevant to my ability to do whatever it is you want me to do?" The question was far more complex than he knew, since I'm sure he wasn't consciously aware of what, exactly, he really wanted me to do, but he answered in the negative.

I didn't get the job, of course. Just as well, I thought. The problem with jobs is that they interfere with life.

I HAD TIME AFTER the interview, since it was suspiciously short, to check out Spoiled Silly. As soon as we pulled into the parking lot, both Kessie and Snookums—I'd gone back home to get them—started drooling. The smell of steak was emanating from the open windows. Seriously?

"Well, no," Zamboni, at reception, explained, "that's just

aromatherapy. We have 'Barbecued Steak' in the diffuser today."

The place had a staff of four. Audrey, a veterinarian, was in charge of the spa part. An ex-veterinarian, she clarified. I suspected an Amber story. So I didn't ask.

"Mostly I do massage, but if I notice something that needs a vet's attention, I'll make a referral," she said.

"Okay, thanks," I said. "Good to know."

Fuchsia was in charge of the salon part. "I'm a fully trained hair stylist, cosmetician, aesthetician, and what have you," she explained, "but I woke up one day and decided I could not, simply would not, continue to feminize women."

"So you feminize dogs?"

"No, I groom them. Sometimes I style them. But I never feminize them. And even if I did," she added, "it wouldn't contribute to their subordination."

I looked doubtful.

"Among other dogs," she clarified.

Okay, point taken. Put a pink bow on an aggressive male rottie and other dogs will still do whatever he says.

TJ was the photographer. She had a box full of props and would reschedule if she didn't have the prop she needed. The one that revealed the inner essence of the dog, she explained. I nodded. And understood completely.

Zamboni took care of everything else. Including aggressive male rotties, with or without pink bows.

I made appointments for everyone.

ON THE FIRST DAY, of those left, Charmaine took Rosie. I'd called to let her know about the place.

I met them there. Mostly because I had nothing better to do.

(What else could possibly *be* better?)

Rosie got a massage. And purred the whole time.

When I told Audrey Rosie's story, she told Zamboni to give Charmaine a lifetime discount coupon.

"You bring her here as often as you want," Audrey said, almost purring herself as she massaged Rosie's fantastic musculature.

And the picture TJ took? It was a perfect surprise: Charmaine's arms around Rosie, her gold medal around Rosie's neck. (But not as perfect as that moment, that first time on the beach—)

ON THE SECOND DAY, Alicia took Jocko. I hadn't seen Jocko since Alicia adopted him, so again I showed up at Spoiled Silly. Jocko was delighted to see me. I was delighted he remembered me.

Jocko decided to try the sauna. It was an infrared sauna, which is better than a regular sauna for dogs, Audrey explained, because they don't make you sweat. And they have all sorts of benefits: they stimulate circulation, increase metabolic activity, strengthen the immune system, regenerate tissue growth. But mostly they just feel good.

"So how's he been?" I asked Alicia, while Jocko lounged in the sauna.

"Fantastic! We quickly exhausted all the routes within a five mile radius of our apartment, so now every morning, before I go to work—there's not much traffic at seven a.m., or many people out and about—we're driving to some other neighborhood and walking for an hour. He *owns* the city," she laughed, scratching his ears.

"An hour every morning?"

"And again every evening. We used to drive to the school yard slash dog park, because you know, they say it's unsafe for a woman to walk at night, but with Jocko— Who's going to be stupid enough to assault a woman with such an escort?" More ear scratching.

TJ certainly captured his happiness, sitting close to Alicia, but as for his inner essence? I preferred to imagine him, his tiger-streaked bulldog boxer body gleaming, strutting the sidewalks of the city with more swagger than Travolta.

ON THE THIRD DAY, I picked up Jan. Biscuit and Cookie had a two o'clock appointment.

Biscuit was quick. His nails took twenty seconds, his bath two minutes, and a towel-dry another minute.

"He's what we call a no-maintenance dog," Fuchsia laughed.

Audrey gave him a thorough going over—I had told her about his recent past and Jan's limited mobility.

In the meantime, Fuchsia dealt with Cookie. Since she was long-haired, she took longer. Plus, once I told Fuchsia about Cookie's past, she decided to pamper her. She got a hydrotherapy bubble bath. And then she pampered her some more. She got a full pawdicure. I agreed that no amount of pampering could make up for what she'd been through. Not even the facial with the cucumber slices.

Jan and I waited in the comfy 'Meditation Room' listening to bamboo flutes and the tinkling waterfall-over-rocks arrangement in the corner, chatting about this and that. We wondered whether the room was for people or dogs. Then we wondered what dogs would dogs meditate about.

"Here they are," Fuchsia handed Biscuit to Jan and Cookie to me. Once they were in our arms, we both sniffed, eyebrows raised.

"I scented Cookie's shampoo with 'Sugar Cookie'," Fuchsia grinned, "and Biscuit got 'Shortbread'."

"Seriously?" We traded and sniffed again. I confess I wanted to take a bite of Biscuit. He really did smell like shortbread!

"Oh, you'd be surprised what we can do here!" she laughed.

TJ took a few cute pictures, one of each of them individually, and then one with the two of them together, but in my virtual photo album? Biscuit's doing figure-eights around Jan's pair of coffee tables, and Cookie's lying on the grass, in the sun, listening to music.

ON THE FOURTH DAY, Tim took Carson. I called ahead to tell them unscented products only, then reminded them again when I got there.

"So how has she been?" I asked Tim while we waited in the Meditation Room. (Fuchsia had taken one look at her luxurious coat and whisked her away.) She was another one I hadn't seen since her adoption.

"She's been great!" he reported. "Ellen did design a special kit for her, we upped the training you'd started, and now she's so good, other hospitals are calling and having us come for the day."

"Really?" I had no idea.

"I'm keeping it fun, though," he said. "No more than three roomfuls a day, ten people, fifteen tops, at a time."

"And she's accurate?"

"From fifty to ninety-eight, depending on the type of cancer."

"Wow." I was truly impressed.

An hour later, Fuchsia presented Carson. Oh my. Instead of a black-and-white spaniel, Carson was now a black-and-pink-and-green spaniel. I had to admit that with the black, it was quite striking. Tim, fortunately, agreed.

TJ came in to get Tim for their photo shoot, and a short while later, I had in my hands a copy of her portrait: she was just sitting, clearly happy, in all her pink and green glory, a stethoscope around her neck.

I SUSPECTED THAT FUCHSIA and TJ were going to go all haute couture with Little Miss, and I suspected that Little Miss would probably enjoy it, so on the fifth day, TJ met me, Sky, and Bo in the field where they played disc every other day.

I'd asked Sky to wear her competition outfit so TJ could get a shot of their final pose—I'd regretted not taking my camera to the competition.

I'd also regretted not taking it to the Sheep Herding Trial, for Hunk's shining moment, but alas, it was too late for that one now.

However, not only did TJ get a perfect picture of Sky and Bo nose to nose, she got several spectacular shots of Bo in action, leaping high, mouth open—athlete-of-the-year stuff. Sky was thrilled. As was I.

ON THE SIXTH DAY, Little Miss had her high fashion makeover. But before that, since I'd taken in Hunk as well, and TJ saw their bond, she took a picture of the two of them together, wearing the collars they'd bought during our first visit to the pet store.

While Hunk relaxed in the jacuzzi, Little Miss was shampooed, and conditionered, and blowdried, and cut, and curled, and styled. And then dressed. The result was, in a word, stunning. Somehow Fuchsia had managed to put gold and scarlet highlights in Little Miss' coat, and with the gold and scarlet taffeta gown—yes, they make gowns for dogs—she looked exquisite. And she knew it. Oh well.

ON THE SEVENTH DAY, I'd booked appointments for Chum and Nisha. He and I waited in the parking lot, so she could walk in with him. After ten minutes, I assumed that Anju had decided not to come. It was sure to be stressful for Nisha—a building she couldn't see, the door, the counter, the tables, as well as people she didn't know and couldn't see wanting to touch her—so I completely understood.

"I guess Nisha's not coming," I said sadly to Chum as I started to lead him inside, but just as I reached out to open the door, he turned abruptly, almost jerking out of my grip.

Nisha!

I recognized Anju's car, but I have to say I almost didn't recognize Nisha when she got out. Yes, she was still a beautiful black lab, it had to be her, but—Anju smiled at my surprise as Nisha led Anju excitedly toward Chum. As *Nisha* led.

"She can see?" I asked with amazement.

"A little bit," Anju replied. "The treatment did have the promised effect, but it's been our daily swims with Chum that have, I think, resulted in the change you're seeing. She has almost all of her confidence and personality back!"

Indeed. Nisha was romping around with Chum, not just standing quietly beside him.

"They do this every morning? At the beach?" I regretted not getting up early enough to join them at least once. Note to self.

"Pretty much!"

TJ had surreptitiously come to the door and gotten a picture of the two of them frolicking, sensing its importance.

"She's still a little insecure when we go for a walk, without Chum there to nudge her, but..." Anju said.

I had an idea. A brilliant idea, if I say so myself. And a week later, I introduced Winn to Nisha.

AND ON THE EIGHTH day, TJ met us at the beach. Both Anju and I now have a perfect picture of Chum and Nisha swimming side by side, broad smiles on their wet faces. (And a soggy beach ball in Chum's mouth.)

I'd taken Hunk as well, hoping TJ could get a shot of him aarfing like a seal, cavorting in the water. I was not disappointed: freeze-framed water droplets all around him, front paws slapping at the surface, he had his mouth open, a Spunky Doo grin on his face that I'd never been close enough to see.

ON THE NINTH DAY, Ange took Amber to Spoiled Silly. There were six other dogs there that day, making for a busy day—they all got spa-ed and salon-ed—and it wasn't until TJ's photograph was presented to me, by Ange, that I understood: Amber was in the middle, the six dogs she'd rescued to date surrounding her.

SPUNKY DOO NEEDED A day all to himself. Correction. Two days. He was shampooed one day, rinsed the next. Not because it took a whole day for Fuchsia to shampoo him. That part took just an hour. (He really likes bubble baths.)

What happened was while he was in the tub, all bubbly, the dog across the room started getting blow-dried. Spunky Doo scrambled out of the tub, skidded toward the dog, then tried to bite the blow dryer. Well, not actually the blow dryer, but the stream of air coming out of the blow dryer.

Then he bit his tongue. Fuchsia bundled him, all soapy and slick, into a towel so Audrey could take a look, and when she did so, she decided that while she was at it she may as well do his teeth. They had a cool untrasound scaler that did a fantastic job without sedation.

Apparently dogs can hear ultrasound. And I guess since Spunky

Doo had never heard sounds at that frequency before, he thought the aliens had landed. Whether he thought they were good aliens or bad aliens wasn't clear, but he *did* think they were aliens worth investigating. If only he could find them. And they *weren't* inside the tooth scaler. He looked there first.

Half an hour later, we had to call in Amber, since the place had become a disaster area and two dogs were missing.

Zamboni tossed Spunky Doo into the Meditation Room with the zen flutes and waterfalls.

We rescheduled.

SO ON THE ELEVENTH day, Spunky Doo got rinsed. Outside. Then dried. With a towel. Outside.

Audrey said she wanted to do some yoga with him. And then cackled.

And then he was turned over to TJ. She had actually gotten several very good shots the day before, but she said she had several costumes and props she wanted to try out with him. I said sure.

No matter what she put on him or with him, he always made us want to laugh. We had a riot. The shot I took home? Spunky Doo in a football helmet, a tutu, and Wonder Woman kneesocks.

AND ON THE TWELFTH day, I took my two. Kessie and Snookums, my two little sweethearts.

"Chicken, turkey, or beef?" Zamboni offered Snookums a jerky treat.

"What, no rabbit? No goose?" I said, laughing. By now, all of the Spoiled Silly staff had heard all about our escapades.

"Venison," he said hopefully.

"Oh god, don't encourage her."

After Spunky Doo, both Audrey and Fuchsia were relieved, I think, to have uneventful sessions with both of them. Kessie liked the massage. Snookums liked the bubble bath. Neither of them liked the blow dryer. Both of them liked the sauna.

As for TJ's photo shoot, she nailed it with Snookums: she'd put her in a camouflage tshirt , then set a pink tiara on her. Inner essence, indeed. (I added it to the picture in my virtual photo album of her in her snuggly, just her little nose sticking out, the tail of a little squeaky mouse protruding from her closed mouth.)

And Kessie. To be honest, it didn't matter what TJ came up with. I will always remember that sweet moment, endlessly repeated, when she'd oh-so-carefully put her ball into my hand, not doubting for an instant that I was paying attention to her, that I would throw it for her (and of course I was, and of course I would) and so, then, she'd crouch, ready—oh-so-ready—